ONE NIGHT

JOANNE RYAN

Tamarillas Press

Cover Design: © Joanne Ryan
ISBN: 978-1-913807-16-0

Other books by Joanne Ryan:
Without Reason
All The Lost Years
Not Your Average Girl
The Lodger
The Double

CHAPTER ONE

Rafe looks so handsome.

The lines of his silver-grey suit show off his tall, athletic build to perfection and the colour highlights his year round tan. His thick dark hair is immaculately styled, save for one stray lock that's fallen over his forehead but rather than detract from his perfection, it only serves to enhance the gorgeousness of him. That lock of hair seems to say, I may be unbelievably attractive but I'm not vain; I haven't noticed that my hair is slightly awry because I'm not obsessed with my appearance. I'm probably the only person here who knows that he deliberately pulls that lock of hair down over his forehead to give that very impression. Contrary to his easy manner and casual friendliness, there is nothing about Rafe that is left to chance, nothing that is not calculated and considered.

The best man leans close to him and whispers something and I see Rafe laugh. I'm too far away to see him closely but I know that the smile will show his perfect teeth and that his piercing blue eyes will crinkle at the corners. He has an open smile which draws the world in and makes everyone want to laugh along with him; he isn't untouchable or aloof as some overly handsome men are. Alain, the best man, has a blonde handsomeness which is equal to Rafe's but he lacks that extra something; that spark that turns a good-looking actor into a superstar.

Not that Rafe is an actor, at least not a paid one.

The wedding guests dressed up in their finery are milling around outside the church chatting and enjoying the weak autumn sunshine and getting in the mood for a good wedding. I take a step further back behind the trunk of the large oak tree directly opposite the church that I'm hiding behind. I want to make sure that there is no possibility of anyone spotting me yet. I lean my back against the trunk and take a deep, shuddering breath to steady my nerves. I grip my handbag tightly to my body as if the action will somehow give me courage. The handbag won't help, but what's inside it most definitely will.

I know a lot of these wedding guests even though they're Rafe's friends and not mine. I imagine their amusement if they were to see me hiding behind a tree and the thought of it is almost enough to make me abandon my plan and run home.

Almost, but not quite.

When I next peer around the tree trunk, Rafe and his best man have gone and the last few guests are slowly making their way through the church entrance. The bride must be on her way. Should I go into the church now or wait until she's arrived and slip in after her? Before I can make up my mind the decision is made for me as the sleek lines of a white limousine pull up in front of the church. I watch as the driver door opens and the chauffeur jumps out quickly and hurries around to the back doors. He adjusts his cap, smooths down his jacket with both hands and then pulls the door open.

She has an absolute meringue of a dress, as I guessed she would. A fairy-tale dress for a beautiful princess. White froth billows from the car as she emerges and her hair is a halo of blondeness, her skin the colour of honey. I gasp as the sun catches the diamonds on her tiara and they sparkle brilliantly.

Or maybe I'm imagining that bit.

She glides up the pathway to the curved arch doorway of the church holding onto her father's arm and I realise that I've completely missed him getting out of the car. I wonder where those minutes went and it feels as if I've time-travelled. I need to move now before it's too late, before the church doors are closed and I've no way of getting in.

I take a deep breath and slip my fingers into my handbag and pull out the bottle of vodka that I purchased on my way here. I had no intention of buying alcohol but when I passed the Co-op at the end of the street, my feet carried me into the shop with a will of their own. A whole six months and three days without drinking, gone, just like that. My good intentions and all of the effort that I made to stop drinking, wasted.

Wasted. Like me.

I swallow down the disgust that I feel with myself and unscrew the top and hold the bottle to my lips and drink. The vodka burns my throat as it goes down and I gag but manage to keep on swallowing until I've drunk it all. As I screw the top back on, I see that there are still a few inches of liquid sloshing around in the bottom. I debate whether to make myself finish it all now but decide not to; I may need it later. I push the bottle down into my large handbag and zip it closed.

I step out from my hiding place and head towards the open church doorway, staggering as I stumble over the uneven grass. My ankle twists painfully and I nearly fall over as one of my heels digs into a divot. Somehow, I manage to remain upright by wind-milling my arms frantically to keep my balance. Once I'm stable a giggle escapes me as I imagine the spectacle that I'm making of myself. I wonder why I'm laughing, because nothing is the slightest bit funny.

As I reach the church, a man in a long, dark robe has come to the church entrance and is beginning to pull the doors closed from the inside. I imagine he's the warden, or something like that. He looks at me in surprise as I slip through the doorway and squeeze past him into the church. Loud organ music is playing and the bride and her father are still making their way down – or should that be up – the aisle to the sounds of the Wedding March. I smile at the warden apologetically as he closes the doors and settle myself on the bone hard seat of the empty back pew. He stares back at me unsmilingly for several moments and I wonder if he knows; if he can detect the smell of vodka on me even though it's supposed to be odourless.

Or perhaps he's just pissed off because I'm late for the wedding; I always read far too much into others' actions and give it far more importance than it deserves. As far as he knows I'm just another guest who's made it to the wedding by the skin of her teeth. I'm dressed to impress in an outfit bought especially for the occasion and the only thing I lack is a hat. Although my dress is white and that's a complete no-no at a wedding.

Which is precisely the reason that I bought it.

The dress is gorgeous and cost a fortune and when I planned this, I imagined Rafe seeing me and regretting what he'd done and the way he'd treated me. I want to take my navy coat off so that the dress is fully on display, but the thought of undoing the buttons and removing it seems complicated and tricky and I think, I know, that I shouldn't have drunk so much. There is a tiny part of me that is still lucid enough to tell me that I should leave right now because this is a very bad and stupid idea and I'm going to regret this so much.

I ignore the feeling.

I direct my gaze down at my feet in case any of the guests in the pew in front decide to turn around to see who the late arrival is. I have no desire to talk to any of them.

The church is large, grand and cavernous and every pew except for the back row is full with expensively dressed guests and I can almost smell the money in the air. I'm sure there must be at least a hundred people in here although I make no attempt to count them. These wedding guests will be the select few; those lucky enough to be in the inner circle of family and close friends. I've no doubt that many hundreds more will be joining the wedding celebrations later on. As I stare down at my feet in their skyscraper heels, I wonder what I would have done if all of the pews had been full. Would I have walked straight back out of the doors again?

I don't know.

The fact that the pew was empty must be a sign.

I swallow down a hiccup and clamp my hand over my mouth; nausea washes over me and I have a sudden urge to vomit. Too late, I realise that I should have eaten something today and then I wouldn't be feeling so sick. I already have the beginnings of a headache and I know that I've overdone the vodka and then immediately think that maybe I should drink the rest because I haven't had enough.

The nasal tones of the vicar interrupt my wandering thoughts and as he begins to speak, I make an effort to concentrate and pay attention. Time jumps around in that weird time-travelling way again and I wonder if I keep falling asleep and then waking up because I'm missing chunks of time. Then I hear him speak the words that seem to be directed straight towards me because they're so clear and loud.

'Should anyone present know of any reason that this couple should not be joined in holy matrimony, speak now or forever hold your peace.' The vicar races through the words as if they're a formality, as if no one could possibly object and even though I never intended doing it, I haul myself up from the seat on shaking legs that seem to have a mind of their own. My handbag crashes to the floor and I feel fear that the vodka bottle will smash which means I'll have to buy another bottle which will mean that I've truly fallen off the wagon. My headache worsens and I grip the back of the pew in front of me to steady myself. Shocked faces turn around to look up at me but I ignore them and turn my head and stare towards the couple at the front of the church. I fix my eyes on the bride and groom who have turned in surprise, surprise which is slowly being replaced by a look of horror gradually spreading across their features.

'I know a reason.' In my head my voice is clear and measured but in reality, it emerges from my mouth as a whisper and the words are slurred. I swallow down the bile that has surged into my mouth and it burns my throat as I loudly repeat the words, almost shouting.

'I know a reason.'

Now I have the attention of everyone in the church and time jumps around again and for one clear moment I realise that I'm making a complete fool of myself. I should stop and leave right now. But the moment disappears in a fog of alcohol and I wipe my shaking hand across my face and my fingers come away wet with tears. I stare in confusion at the streaks of black on my fingers before realising that it's the mascara that I applied so carefully this morning.

'It should have been me!' I shout through sobs, as I stare at Rafe. 'You should have been marrying me!'

CHAPTER TWO

It got to half-past-ten before we all believed what everyone had been praying for; Evelyn would not be coming into the office today. Such is Evelyn's power and importance, she didn't feel the need to actually speak to anyone in the department that she manages. The news came from HR who sent a round robin email to the entire team. Once the email hit our inboxes I could feel the atmosphere palpably change and everyone visibly relaxed; today was going to be a good day, the sort of day we could have every day if we didn't have a psychopath for a boss.

I breathed a huge sigh of relief, not least because I'm still suffering from a massive hangover from my vodka binge on Saturday. If I worked for anyone else but Evelyn I would have called in sick but there was no way I could do that with her. Evelyn doesn't agree with her staff being off sick, that privilege is reserved for her and her alone. According to Evelyn's rules, no one else but her is ever *really* ill, they're simply skiving. Pretty much the same rule applies to working from home. Company policy is that a reasonable request to work from home should be granted, but not in this office.

'Fucking result, eh?' Jack asks from his desk directly opposite me.

I laugh, which hurts my head so I stop.

'Brilliant,' I say. 'I wonder what's wrong with her?'

'Probably fuck all,' Jack says, standing up and stretching his arms high above his head and yawning loudly. 'Maybe we've got lucky and she's died. I'm going out for a smoke, you coming out for a chat?'

'Got to finish this,' I lie, nodding at my screen.

He shrugs and near-sprints to the end of the office, opens the door and disappears into the corridor. He'll be having a cigarette break every hour now that Evelyn's not in and as I look around the office there's an almost party-like feel to the place. Instead of the usual frowns of concentration and everyone hunched over their desks, my work colleagues are chatting with each other and looking relaxed. The work will get done just the same as it always does but without the element of fear and bullying.

I contemplate getting myself a coffee but quickly decide not to because I think that I might just vomit it straight back up. Yesterday I felt so ill that I couldn't even keep sips of water down. I suppose I'm lucky that I'm still alive and haven't died from alcohol poisoning considering that I drank an entire large bottle of vodka. I deserve to feel bad, because I didn't just fall off the wagon, I jumped off with both feet and did a swan dive for good measure.

And that's without remembering what I did.

I wince at the bits that I do recall; standing up in the church and screaming at Rafe and his bride, being ejected from the church by the warden and several of Rafe's friends whilst screaming and sobbing. There is a brief snapshot in my head of being in a taxi going God knows where and talking absolute drivel to the taxi driver whilst imagining that I was making brilliant conversation. Time jumps again to me shouting and waving my arms around at someone, although I have no idea who that someone was. My final drunken time-travel was to find myself slumped on a bench in a park that I've never been to before, where I awoke to darkness and my watch telling me that it was nearly eleven o'clock at night. Eight hours had elapsed since I'd arrived at the church for Rafe's wedding and I had no idea where I'd been or what I'd been doing for all of that time. I was freezing-cold, my coat was nowhere to be seen, one of the heels was missing from one of my shoes and to my absolute shame, I'd wet myself. Thankfully, my handbag was underneath my head as I'd been using it as a pillow so at least I hadn't lost it. Although the empty bottle of vodka was smashed into pieces and everything, including me, stank of vodka and urine.

I have no idea how I got there and I won't be trying very hard to remember. Some things, as I know from experience, are best not remembered.

I feel utterly disgusted and ashamed of myself and the only good thing about it is that I don't remember most of what happened after I stood up at the wedding. I should feel bad about crashing Rafe's wedding but I don't; he deserved it. For what he did, disrupting his wedding day was nothing. The thing I do feel bad about is the fact that I drank a whole bottle of vodka and made a complete and utter fool of myself. My intention had been to sit in the church and make sure that Rafe saw me looking utterly stunning so he could see what he was missing. I'd be dignified and aloof and he'd feel guilty for treating me like shit and also a little regretful at what he was giving up.

I think my plan failed spectacularly on both counts.

I would never have gone through with it if I hadn't been wasted and I don't know why I ever kidded myself that I would. I think I always knew I was going to buy that vodka and I just pretended to myself that I wasn't. Maybe I made the whole plan up just so I could have a drink; who knows? I gave up drinking alcohol because of my behaviour. I wasn't an alcoholic but I never knew when to stop and I could never have just one drink, it was all or nothing. What would start out as a great evening would descend into drunken embarrassment followed by huge lumps, if not all, of the evening's events missing from my memory. Rafe likes to tell everyone that my drinking was the reason we split up but it wasn't, because the drinking only began *after* he started cheating on me.

Not that anyone who was at the wedding will believe that now. The only consolation is that I'll never see any of them again because they move in very different circles to me.

'Cheer up, mate.' Jack's back and he slumps into his swivel chair in a cloud of tobacco-ed air and spins the chair around in circles.

'Bit of a headache,' I say, with a grimace.

'Heavy weekend, was it?' Jack asks.

'No,' I lie. 'Got a sore throat as well so I think I've picked up a bug.'

I'm not lying, I do have a sore throat. Although it's not a bug, I've burned it from drinking neat vodka.

'Go home,' he says, airily. 'Bitch face isn't here to stop you.'

'No,' I say, looking at my screen to signal an end to the conversation. 'I'll be fine.'

'Whatevs.' Jack shrugs. I've pissed him off by not wanting to talk and I feel momentarily bad but then stop myself. I feel like shit and I don't feel like talking and as far as he knows I'm not feeling well. We're good mates and he'll get over it. I may even tell him what I did one day, when I feel able to laugh about it. Jack won't judge me because he knows what happened with Rafe and he hates him on my behalf.

I don't hate Rafe. Although I tell myself I do.

I tap a few keys and keep my gaze on the screen to give the pretence of working and this is how I spend the rest of the morning. I badly want to go home and lie down and die but I won't; not least because I'll have to explain myself to Evelyn when she comes in tomorrow or whenever she comes back to the office. I'm not up to that; I already have the horrible feeling that I'm going to be her new victim but on the remote chance that I'm not, I'm doing my very best to be a model employee.

There are thirty-eight of us working in this office, a week ago there were thirty-nine. Sasha used to sit at the desk nearest the door but she phoned HR first thing last Monday morning and tendered her resignation.

None of us were even slightly surprised.

It was only a matter of time before she couldn't take any more; she put up a bit of a fight at first but soon gave up. The outcome was inevitable because you can't win with a psychopath, or maybe Evelyn's a sociopath, I'm not sure which of them she is but she's definitely one of them.

The office was quiet after Evelyn came out of her office and made the announcement about Sasha. She didn't beat about the bush but simply announced that Sasha had left for *personal reasons* and that HR would be seeking a replacement for her as soon as possible. She then stood and looked around at everyone and I wondered if someone was going to challenge her and say something. No one did. Once Evelyn had returned to her office and closed the door, my thirty-seven work colleagues silently returned to their screens and continued their work.

None of us could even look at each other. Whilst I'd like to think that it was because we were ashamed that yet another of our colleagues has been bullied out of the company, I knew that the reason wasn't shame, but fear.

Fear that now that Sasha had gone, Evelyn would be looking for a new victim to pick on and everyone was thinking the same thing.

I hope it's not me.

Evelyn's very clever; to look at her you wouldn't think she's a bully because her manner doesn't give it away and that's her strength, because no one outside of this office ever suspects. Her line manager is the Director of Marketing and he's a placid, easy going man who doesn't micro-manage and is happy to leave his managers to manage their own teams. He's a great boss and Evelyn gets on very well with him and he thinks the sun shines out of her arse. He rarely comes into the office because it runs so well, although when he does visit he has a nice chat with everyone because he's that sort of guy.

The trouble is, standing between all of us in the office and him is Evelyn, so to get to him you have to go through her. It's impossible, and the one person who tried to jump over her and go straight to the Director and speak to him about Evelyn received short shrift. The whole department were asked if there was a problem in the office with Evelyn and of course everyone said no, because who wants to put their neck on the line? And that was the end of that. And the would-be whistle-blower; well, she was marked down as a liar and a malicious trouble-maker and she left the company soon afterwards.

Evelyn has honed her bullying skills to perfection over the years and once she has her hooks into you, it's impossible to break free. She starts by taking a special interest in your development and will set tasks for you to complete. Easy enough tasks; except that she demands a hundred-percent success rate and when you don't achieve this immediately she'll chip away at your confidence by implying that other people don't have a problem doing so. The failure to hit the required percentage means being put on a performance plan which entails being helped to reach the targets. In reality this results in the victim being so paralysed with the fear of making a mistake that they have no hope of hitting any target, ever. Even if the victim somehow passes this first test they won't survive because Evelyn will find that they have a negative attitude to work. Their failure to agree that they have a negative attitude is used as the very proof of their negativity and non-team-like positivity. It's a bit like the old witch trials; survive the ducking stool and it proves you're a witch, drown and you're innocent. In other words, you can't win. In my three years here I've seen one other victim leave before Sasha but I've been told that there were many others before. The victim before Sasha refused to give their notice in but the end result was the same because they were sacked after being off on sick leave for six months with depression.

I had no idea of any of this when I started at the company. When I came for my interview I thought that Evelyn was *nice*; in her fifties, she seemed friendly and down to earth. I didn't give her that much thought because I'm just a minion and I thought I'd have very little contact with her.

Which was true.

Until now.

Since Sasha left, Evelyn has called me into her office several times and I see the pattern that was meted out to Sasha being repeated with me. She's started to show a special interest in me and has set me a special task to complete. I have no idea why I've been selected. According to my colleagues who've worked here for years, there is no typical victim; male, female, young or old, there is no type. I hope I'm wrong about it being my turn but I don't think that I am.

I stare unseeingly at the screen and wonder why life can be wonderful and then one day it's not and before you know it, your whole life has turned to shit. Unsurprisingly, the screen stares back at me and doesn't answer.

Hoots of laughter from the other end of the office draw my attention and I look up to see several of my colleagues crowded around Darla's desk.

'She's showing them her hen do photos,' Jack says, looking over at me.

I raise an eyebrow and he smirks.

'I've already seen them,' he says. 'And I can tell you she's a right filthy cow. Her new husband's got his work cut out with her.'

I laugh, despite my thumping head and Jack joins in.

'That's better,' he says. 'We've got to make the most of having a day without that cow, don't want to waste it being miserable and actually doing some fucking work.'

I am miserable, there's no denying it, but I paste on a smile because he's right, we should make the most of the fact that Evelyn's not here. One person shouldn't be able to dictate the lives of every person in a large office but Evelyn does. When I wonder how that can possibly be, I remind myself that Hitler managed to do it very well on a much larger scale as have many other psychopaths.

'So, I'm thinking,' Jack says, stretching his long, gangly legs out as he leans back in his chair so that his feet jut out in front of the desk. 'That I should go and get a Maccy D's for lunch to sort out your headache and a chocolate milk shake for your sore throat. What do you say? My treat.'

The thought of a burger and chips makes me want to hurl but I can't rebuff him again. Kill or cure, I suppose. Maybe I'll feel better if I eat something and then throw up.

'That would be great,' I lie. 'But you don't have to pay for me, let me treat you for a change.'

'Nope, my treat.' Jack jumps up from his chair and looks at his watch. 'It's five-to-twelve so that's near enough to lunchtime for me. Cheeseburger or chicken nuggets?' he asks.

Before I can answer he hurriedly flops back down in his seat, shoves his feet underneath the desk and stares at his screen. This is the reaction usually caused by the appearance of Evelyn so I look down the office fully expecting to see her heading our way but it's Gareth Heath, the Marketing Director, who's just come in. I honestly think that Jack has a sixth sense because Gareth has hardly got through the door. I wonder if someone at the other end of the office will tell him that Evelyn isn't in today or if it'll be left to me or Jack because we're the closest to Evelyn's office door. I'm surprised that he doesn't already know, especially as HR managed to send us all an email; that's one big black mark for HR. Gareth stops in the centre of the office and looks around expectantly.

'Everyone,' he says, hesitantly. 'Could I have your attention, please?'

He doesn't really need to ask because everyone is already looking at him.

'Okay.' He clears his throat and looks down at the floor before looking back up. 'There's no easy way to say this so I'll just come right out and say it. A terrible thing has happened and I'm sorry to have to tell you that Evelyn has passed away.'

The office is totally silent as we all take in the shock news. Chrissie, whose desk is right in front of where Gareth is standing, stares at him in open-mouthed shock before asking in a shaky voice.

'Oh my God, that's terrible. What happened?'

'I'm sorry,' Gareth says. 'But I can't tell you any more than that at this time. I know this will have come as a massive shock to you all as it has to me and I think it would be best if you all finish for today and go home now.'

He makes his way slowly to the door, stopping on the way when some of my colleagues speak to him. I think they're asking what happened because each time he shakes his head and I wonder why they're asking when he's just told us that he doesn't have any more details.

I look across at Jack and he's already closing down his PC and sweeping his pens and papers in his open drawer. I turn my screen off and shove the file that I've been staring at for hours back into the tray. People are wasting no time in putting their coats on and making ready to leave now that Gareth has gone.

'Well,' Jack says, standing up and shrugging on his jacket. 'That's what you call a result.'

'Jack!' I say, in a telling-off voice.

'Ding, dong,' he says, his face breaking into a huge smile and doing a double thumbs up at me. 'The fucking bitch is dead.'

CHAPTER THREE

I was looking forward to getting home early and crashing in bed for the rest of the day but it's not to be. As I'm about to put my key in the front door it's pulled open by Olivia, my flatmate. Olivia's perfect face is marred by double frown lines between her brows and my heart sinks. I'm definitely not in the mood to put up with her. Why isn't she at work? She steps outside and deposits a bag of rubbish on the doormat where it will sit until one of us takes it down to the communal dustbins, before speaking to me.

'What are you doing here?' she asks, echoing my thoughts.

'Half-day holiday,' I lie, as I follow her into the hallway. 'You?'

She twists her mouth into a grimace. 'I was owed some time so thought I'd catch up on my laundry from the weekend. Unfortunately, the washing machine has other ideas.'

I look through the kitchen doorway to see a man

crouched over the washing machine, an open bag of tools by his side.

'I called Jed and he very kindly fitted us in before his next job,' Olivia says. She steps into the kitchen and I feel duty bound to follow her.

'Anything for you, my darling,' Jed drawls from the floor.

'So lucky to have a friend who's an engineer,' Olivia simpers. 'Otherwise we'd be waiting weeks to get it fixed.'

I nod as if I care and am about to escape to my bedroom when Jed holds his hand up in the air and shouts. 'Here's the little bugger!' He scrambles up off the floor to show his prize to Olivia.

'What.' Olivia wrinkles her nose as she scrutinises it. 'Is that?'

Jed turns the item around in his hand and rubs his finger over it.

'Not completely sure but it looks like a flattened screw-top cap from a bottle.'

Olivia looks at me and I stare back at her without blinking.

'Do you know anything about this?' Olivia asks, in an accusing tone. 'Did you use the washing machine at the weekend?'

'No, I did not,' I say, slightly indignantly. 'Like you, I intended catching up on my washing today.'

'But that's not the real problem,' Jed interrupts. 'Your real problem is the glass.'

'The glass?' Olivia looks at him.

'Yeah, looks like broken glass from a bottle.

Trouble is, it's cut the outlet pipe when the machine emptied so you're going to need a new one fitted.'

'How on earth did a bottle get in there?' Olivia demands.

'Who knows,' Jed says, with a shrug. 'It's not a whole bottle, just a bit of glass. There could have been more and it pumped out when the machine emptied but this bit was too big. I'll do you a special price though, so no worries. It's an easy fix.'

Olivia folds her arms and frowns and I decide that now is a good time to retreat to my bedroom.

'Let me know my share of the cost, Olivia,' I say, as I turn to walk back out into the hallway and along to my bedroom. 'And I'll ping you the money.'

She stares at me for a moment and cocks her head to one side and narrows her eyes. It's not a good look on such a beautiful woman and I'm almost tempted to tell her so.

'Are you sure you don't know anything about this, Josephine?'

I ignore her, and the fact that she's used my full name, which I hate, and walk towards the door. She calls me by my full name to annoy me because I dared to once call her Olive for a joke.

'Because it's funny how it happened while only you were here,' she adds.

I stop mid-walk and turn to face her, giving her my best thousand-yard-death-stare.

'I don't know about you, Olivia, but I'm not in

the habit of washing glass with my clothes. I have no idea how it got there, but I do know that it's nothing to do with me. I haven't used the washing machine all weekend so maybe *you* did it last week.' I turn on my heel and with my nose in the air, exit the kitchen.

I stomp down the hallway and despite feeling like death warmed up, I can't help smirking to myself.

I'm such a liar.

* * *

There is a school of thought that says if you can't sleep you should get up and do something useful instead of lying there worrying about not sleeping. Getting up and doing something doesn't help you to sleep any better, but at least you're making use of the time instead of lying in bed staring at the ceiling.

So now, instead of lying in bed and tossing and turning and running everything around in my head, I get out of bed and go and sit in the lounge by the window. It's hardly doing anything useful but it beats lying in bed in the darkness. I don't put any lights on because I don't want to wake Olivia. She's a very light sleeper and the merest hint of light or noise will wake her. I woke her once simply by turning the kettle on.

I'm very considerate, aren't I?

Not really; I don't care whether I disturb her

but I don't want her questioning why I'm awake and looking at me with her doll-like eyes because I just might forget myself and punch her in the face. She seems to think that because she owns this flat, she has some sort of control over me and my life. I pay rent, Olivia, so butt out. Thank God that she was away over the weekend so wasn't here to witness my drunken antics. I've no doubt that if she had been here, I would've been asked to move out immediately after I'd arrived home stinking of vodka and urine. And that wouldn't have been the worst of it; I'm an unpleasant drunk and all the horrible things that I normally stop myself from saying come blurting out when I'm wasted. No doubt I'd have slapped her for good measure, too, so she actually had a very lucky escape.

Obviously, it was me who broke the washing machine but no way am I going to confess to Olivia. Who knows why I decided to put a wash on when I arrived back here on Saturday night? I stuffed my dress, underwear and handbag into the washing machine and put it on a hot wash. If I hadn't lost my coat, no doubt that would have gone in there, too. I don't remember doing it and I didn't even realise I'd done it until Sunday night when I noticed the washing machine light blinking at me. Although I was aware enough to empty out the contents of my handbag, I must have missed some glass and the bottle top from the broken bottle.

When I pulled it all out of the washing machine,

I stuffed it into a bin liner and put it in the bottom of my wardrobe. I'm never going to wear the dress again so I have no idea why I bothered washing it. The handbag was quite a nice one but after a hot wash the edges had frayed and it had gone all misshapen. I threw the shoes in with it all because a shoe with a heel missing isn't much use. I'll be putting it all in the dustbin when I'm feeling normal enough to make a visit to the communal bins.

I sigh and look out of the window and the empty street below. I only managed to fall asleep last night because I deliberately watched TV until very late, but I could still only stay asleep for a few hours. When I woke at three I knew there was no way I'd be going back to sleep because my brain felt like it was on fire. I was the same on Sunday night and I only slept on Saturday night because I was practically unconscious. By Sunday the disgust and regret had started to kick in and that's what's been keeping me awake. After a binge, I have weird dreams and I'm never sure if they're things that I've actually done on one of my blackouts, or if they're nightmares that my brain has made up. I start to panic about what I might have done and I lie there petrified waiting for the retribution that will surely arrive.

I really need to sort my life out and get a place to live that doesn't have an Olivia in it. Olivia's flat is on the second floor of a block of smart apartments in the centre of town. She has the bigger bedroom and we share the kitchen and lounge. Olivia's room has an ensuite, so in theory the main bathroom is mine but in reality, if she has her friends over they always use *my* bathroom and not hers. I try not to feel pissed off about it but I am. I've considered putting a padlock on the door to stop her friends using it but have stopped myself from doing so because Olivia will imply that I'm making a fuss about nothing. She's barely tolerable on a normal day let alone when I have to actually speak to her. Olivia's go-to answer to any sort of criticism is an arch of her perfect eyebrows and a *what's all the fuss about* look. She professes to be laid back but it's not her bathroom that's being used by other people, is it? How would she like it if I invited Jack over and he went and took a massive shit in her ensuite?

I never have invited Jack or any of my other friends over because I wouldn't feel comfortable with Olivia here. I don't feel as if I can relax with her around. Besides which, I drifted away from most of my friends when I met Rafe because they *weren't his type of people,* as he put it, so I can hardly go back and hook up with them again just because Rafe and I are no longer together. Rafe thought my friends were common, and, as it turned out, he thought I was common, too, but he didn't decide to tell me that until he dumped me.

So really, Jack is my only proper friend at the moment, although I have been out with some of the crowd from work but that was a long time ago. Part of me knows that only having one friend is not healthy and I really need to do something about it.

Olivia and I are not in any way friends; she advertised for a flat-mate to help with her mortgage, I applied, the rent was acceptable and I moved in. We don't dislike each other or anything, we're just very different people.

Okay, actually, yes, I do dislike her, although I've tried not to.

And maybe I'm a little bit jealous of her too.

She's pretty in that feminine way that some girls are without even trying. I've never seen her look a mess, even when I've seen her in the morning and she's obviously just got out of bed, she still looks perfect. I shouldn't think she ever has to shave her legs or pluck her eyebrows because she's naturally beautiful in that pale blonde sort of way. But it's not her perfect looks that make me dislike her – although she does look a bit like Rafe's new wife – it's the way she talks to me as if I'm beneath her. She has no sense of humour and stares at me blankly whenever I've tried to make a joke about anything so I don't bother trying anymore. I don't think we're on the same wavelength about anything and whenever our paths cross, I feel as if I'm sharing a flat with a Stepford wife or one of my old school teachers.

When I told Jack what she was like, he said I could move in with him if I wanted to and I am sorely tempted. But the fact that we're such good mates stops me, because I'm afraid that living together might spoil that. It could be great fun living with Jack but I suppose I just don't want to take the chance that it could all go wrong and we wouldn't be friends anymore.

Also, he has a balcony and lives on the sixth floor.

I have a fear of heights which I can just about cope with as long as there are solid walls around me. Balconies give me the heebie-jeebies and I could never stand on one, but worse than that, I can't sit in a room if the door to one is open. This, along with all the other reasons, is why I'm still at Olivia's. I tell myself that I don't have to see her very much because I have a TV in my room for when she's here so there's no need to spend any time at all with her. I've never seen her eat breakfast because she barely eats so she can stay super-thin and she's out most evenings because there's always a man chasing her. It's annoying when she is here and has her friends around because I feel that I have to stay in my room. I'm not sure if I imagine it but all of her friends look at me in a strange way and I think she must have told them that I'm weird or something. She always forewarns me if any of them are coming over so she obviously doesn't want me around.

I'm sorely tempted to take the toilet roll and towels out of my bathroom the next time she invites her friends over to make it awkward for them to use it.

Anyway, here I am, sitting in the armchair that looks out over the street and the block of flats opposite, trying to stop the total embarrassment of my antics last Saturday from whirling through my head. This was one of the main reasons that I stopped drinking six months ago. It's all very well making a dick of myself and stumbling around like the town drunk, but what about the bits that I can't remember? What if I did something really bad and I have no knowledge of it?

When I told Jack that this was the reason why I wasn't drinking anymore, he thought it was hilarious. What could be better, he said, that doing something bad and having no memory of it? The way he sees it, if I can't remember what I did then I don't have to feel guilty about it.

But I don't feel like that; I don't like having big black voids of nothingness, it makes me feel out of control.

Which brings me back to Saturday.

I *do* remember shouting at someone; I mean *really* shouting and being aggressive, which isn't unusual because like I've said, I'm an unpleasant drunk. And really, shouting at someone is nothing compared to crashing and attempting to wreck a wedding, is it? Except that it's much worse, because I now remember who it was I was shouting at.

It was Evelyn.

CHAPTER FOUR

I feel so tired but somehow manage to crawl into work on Tuesday. The irony isn't lost on me that now Evelyn is dead I could call in sick without fear of reprisals.

But I don't.

I don't want to be alone with my thoughts all day because last night was bad enough.

After remembering that Evelyn was the person I was shouting at on Saturday night, all my selfish brain can tell me is that it's okay because she's dead now and no one will ever know. Unless she's told someone, of course, which sends me down a rabbit-hole of wondering when she died and whether she told anyone before whatever it is killed her, happened. I'm assuming she had a heart attack or maybe a car accident because it must been sudden, so did she even have a chance to tell anyone? Has she reported me to the police for threatening behaviour? I don't know if I was threatening but I was definitely wasted and definitely aggressive. I can only remember snapshots of it but I do recall telling her that I wasn't going to stand for her bullying. I can also hear myself saying she had to stop or else I'd make her.

It seemed like a good idea at the time, the same way as standing up at Rafe's wedding seemed like a good idea but I was absolutely smashed and not thinking straight. They were both two of the most stupid things I've ever done. There is no doubt in my mind that if Evelyn wasn't dead, she would have sacked me the very minute I turned up at work on Monday morning. So all that's going through my mind is that Evelyn being dead has been very convenient for me and let me off the hook and what sort of person does that make me?

Not a very nice one.

I can't pretend that I'm sorry she's dead, because I'm not. She was a horrible person, a bully who made her employee's lives miserable and I'm positive that she won't be missed by one single person in that office. But that doesn't make my being nasty and aggressive to her any more justifiable.

As if crashing Rafe's wedding wasn't enough, haranguing Evelyn is another reason why I shouldn't ever drink again. Even though I'm not, nor have I ever been, an alcoholic, I *am* a binge drinker and a nasty drunk so I need to steer well clear of alcohol in the future. This time, it has to be for good and not just for six months.

Just to satisfy myself that I didn't fit the profile of an alcoholic, I looked up the definition and this is what it said;

Alcoholism is defined by alcohol dependence, which is the body's physical inability to stop drinking and the presence of alcohol cravings.

So I'm not an alcoholic because I stopped drinking easily and never touched a drop for over six months and most of the time, I didn't even miss it.

So why do I want a drink now when it's only nine-thirty in the morning?

'Well,' Jack says, loudly from the desk opposite. 'Considering our illustrious leader is no more, you're pretty fucking miserable.'

'I'm fine,' I say, my head down, pretending to type.

'You want to tell your face that because I don't think it got the memo.'

I look up to see Jack staring across at me thoughtfully and I decide that I can't keep all of this bottled up. I need to tell someone because I'm driving myself mad with it whirling around and around in my head. Maybe if I tell Jack and get it off my chest, I'll feel a bit better. He'll probably laugh and tell me not to worry about it, if I know him.

'I need to talk to you about something,' I say, quietly, glancing around the office to see if anyone is looking at us. Of course, no one is, I'm just paranoid. 'But not here.'

'Let's go out for lunch,' Jack says, with a wink.

'And you can tell uncle Jack all about it.'

* * *

'So you went to her house?' Jack asks, stirring his coffee.

We're sat in a booth at *Florrie's Cafe*, a place off the high street which is frequented by little old ladies and mums with screaming babies lassoed into pushchairs. This isn't a place for office-types go for lunch so no one who knows me is likely to be in here eavesdropping on us.

I told you I was paranoid.

'I don't know.' Everyone in our department knows where Evelyn lives; she was always bragging about her big house and how posh her street was and made no secret of her address, so I *could* have gone there but I can't remember.

'Okay. Were you inside somewhere or outside in the street?'

I shrug.

'Fucking hell,' Jack says, blowing through his teeth. 'You really were smashed.'

'I know,' I say, 'I can only remember bits of it. I do remember being in a cab so maybe I got one to her house but I honestly don't know. The cab could have been after I saw her. I might have bumped into her in the street or knocked on her door, I really have no idea.'

Jack looks at me and snorts and starts laughing again.

'What?' I demand.

'Sorry,' he says, between snorts. 'I just wish I'd been there.'

I stare at him.

'You know, when you crashed the wedding. Wish I'd seen that prick Rafe's face.' He snorts again and wipes tears from his eyes and I sit back with a sigh and fold my arms and wait for him to get it out of his system.

I do feel better for telling him, though, despite feeling like an absolute fool. I've given him all of the details bar the fact that I wet myself because some things definitely don't need to be shared.

'Come on, Josie, you have to admit it is a *bit* funny.'

'Yeah, I suppose it is. A bit.' I feel my lips twitch. 'Although I would have found it a lot funnier if it had been someone else doing it and not me.'

'So,' he eventually says, composing himself. 'You tracked her down and gave her what for and then somehow found yourself asleep on a park bench?'

'Yep.'

'And what happened after that? Where did you go then?'

'Back to my flat. I had no idea where I was so I had to Google map it. It was some big park over the other side of town that I'd never been to before.'

'Was it close to Evelyn's house?'

'No, not really, a couple of miles, God knows how I managed to get there. Once I got out of the park I called a cab and went home.' I cringe as I remember the cab driver wrinkling his nose as I got into the car. I don't even remember getting into my flat or going to bed.

'Hmm.' He looks thoughtful. 'I'd forget about it if I were you because she's dead now and even if she told someone about it, so what? Getting drunk and giving someone a mouthful isn't exactly an offence, so what's the point in worrying about it? I wish I'd known she was going to die because I'd have told her what I thought of her and so would lots of other people.'

'I feel a bit bad, though,' I say.

'Why?' he asks. 'Because she's dead? She was a vile bitch and the world is better off without her. Don't waste your time feeling sorry about it.'

'You make it sound so easy,' I say.

'It is. She deserved it, you were the new victim and she was going to make your life unbearable. Rafe and his stuck-up bride deserved it. Job done. Move on. Don't waste any more time thinking about any of them.'

Jack does his double thumbs up thing again and I can't help laughing.

'I always feel better talking to you,' I say.

'Glad to help,' he says. 'You should come flat-share with me instead of staying with that snooty ice-queen and I'd soon teach you to stop feeling guilty about pointless shit.'

'Don't tempt me,' I say.

'But you'd have to promise not to put any vodka bottles in the washing machine because some things are a step too far.' He laughs to show me he's joking.

'That will never happen again,' I state, with certainty. 'Because I'm never drinking again. That was the very last time. I can't cope with the hangovers or the blackouts.'

'Right, now we've got that sorted, let's celebrate with one of *Florrie's* big fat cakes.' Jack gets up and goes to the counter and when he returns he has two giant iced doughnuts. He puts one in front of me and slides onto the bench opposite.

'The waitress says it's table service only but she's let me have them just this once.' Jack picks up his doughnut and scrutinises it before taking an enormous bite. 'I gave her my best smile and she was putty in my hands.'

I bite into the doughnut and it's delicious. I've hardly eaten since Saturday as I haven't been able to keep anything down but now I'm suddenly ravenous. Maybe it's the unburdening it all onto Jack; they do say a trouble shared is a trouble halved. I take giant bites from the doughnut and shovel it down in seconds, feeling like a complete pig.

'We'd better get a move on,' I say, with a mouthful of doughnut as I look at my watch. 'Or else we're going to be late back.'

'Who gives a shit,' Jack replies. 'We're boss-less at the moment so let's make the most of it.'

He's got a point.

Jack waves at the waitress and she scurries over

and he orders two more coffees and because I have a lot of catching up to do, I order a cheese toastie to go with it. She takes a long time writing the order down in her old-school notepad and I think maybe Jack's *special smile* has worked its magic on her. I sometimes forget that Jack is good-looking in a rangy, laid-back sort of way because we're such good mates that I don't ever look at him in *that* way.

Jack starts scrolling on his phone so I pick mine up, switch Facebook accounts and scroll to Rafe's Facebook page. He blocked me a long time ago but I created a fake profile so I can still see what he's doing. My fake profile isn't a friend of his but he's such a show off that he won't make his profile private. There's a picture on his feed of him and his new wife, Jacinta, in their wedding finery looking sickeningly happy. There are also what seem like hundreds of pictures of a deserted beach in the Maldives where they're spending their honeymoon. The pictures have hundreds of likes and I feel evil just looking at them; why does he get to have a happy ending and I don't? Is it my fault that I wasn't born into a rich, posh family like his? I was good enough to share his life and bed for over a year but not good enough to settle down with.

I should stop looking; the first time I looked I was afraid that I was going to be slagged off and made a laughing stock all over Facebook for crashing their wedding. When I looked and I didn't even get a mention, I was strangely disappointed.

Maybe Rafe's right; maybe I am *not right in the head*, as he was so fond of saying.

'Shit.' Jack is staring at his phone, his face serious.

'What?' I ask.

He doesn't speak but frowns and studies his phone.

'What?' I ask again, starting to feel uneasy.

'Okay,' he says, slowly. 'Don't panic because it doesn't change anything.'

'Why would I panic?'

He's silent and I make to grab his phone and he throws me a warning look and I realise that my voice has become very loud. A little old lady and two mums with buggies have turned to stare at us with interest. Jack gives them a warm smile and then the waitress appears with our coffees and my toastie and makes a big fuss about putting them on the table and turning them around the right way. She smiles at Jack and spends a long time getting his cup straight, because she obviously fancies him, and I want to scream at her to *fuck off* so Jack can tell me what it is that I don't need to panic about.

The minute she's gone I look at Jack and he stares back at me unsmilingly and I dread what he's going to say. I stare down at my cheese toastie and my appetite has vanished and I feel a sense of impending doom descend over me.

''So,' he says, leaning across the table and dropping his voice to just above a whisper. 'If

Evelyn told anyone what you did on Saturday, you might be getting asked some awkward questions so you're going to need to prepare for that.' He passes his phone to me and I stare at the screen. It's the front page of the local online newspaper and as I read it, my head starts to hurt and the doughnut that I've just eaten has turned into a lead weight in my stomach.

Local career-woman found beaten to death, the headline splashed across the screen reads.

Underneath the headline is a picture of Evelyn.

CHAPTER FIVE

I don't know how I got through the rest of the day at work. Once I'd seen the news about Evelyn, all I wanted to do was to go straight home and hide in my bedroom and wish that Saturday never happened.

Jack talked me out of it; he said that I'd done nothing wrong and running away and hiding was not the answer. I needed to carry on as usual, he said, because if the police did know that I'd seen Evelyn before she died, if I was hiding away it would look suspicious.

Of course, as soon as we walked into the office, all that anyone could talk about was Evelyn being murdered. The shock on everyone's face was genuine but there was also a feeling of barely hidden excitement that someone we know had been murdered. No one even pretended to be sad about Evelyn or the way she died. I stopped and chatted to people as we made our way into the office and according to Jack, I appeared perfectly normal.

I'm obviously a much better actress than I thought.

When I eventually sat down at my desk, I pretended to work but really I was searching the internet for details of Evelyn's murder and I suspect that everyone else was, too. Details were scant and the police weren't sure exactly when she was murdered. The horrible part of me hoped that it was before she had a chance to tell anyone that I'd spoken to her.

But what if someone saw me? I don't know where I was when I was shouting at her; it could have been a public place for all I know. For once, I wish I could remember exactly what I'd done because if it was a public place it's just a matter of time before the police turn up at my door.

What if they suspect me?

Obviously, I didn't murder her but that's not to say that I didn't wish her dead, many, many times. And don't the police treat everyone like a suspect until they're ruled out? There won't be any evidence against me but I don't relish the thought of being questioned and treated as a criminal.

Although, what if I slapped Evelyn? It's quite possible because it wouldn't be the first time that I'd let rip at someone when I was wasted. Could there could be evidence linking me to her even though I never murdered her, could DNA from my hand be found on her face? I honestly don't know.

What a mess.

And even if I didn't slap her and there isn't any evidence, if the police somehow do know about me seeing Evelyn, word will get around the office about what I did, which means that word will get out about crashing Rafe's wedding.

It would be utterly mortifying.

When I voiced all this to Jack in the cafe, he laughed and said *own it, girl* and *enjoy it,* because it just makes me a more interesting person and it's hilarious. Besides which, he said, every person in that office hated Evelyn's guts and they'll be jealous that they didn't get to give her a mouthful before she died.

But I don't think the police will quite see it that way.

Or HR.

Or Gareth Heath.

Every time I heard the main office door open, my heart would start to pound and I'd look up expecting to see uniformed police coming in to question me. They didn't appear but Gavin Heath, the Marketing Director did. He looked very solemn and everyone stopped what they were doing – surfing the net, most likely – and waited for him to make his way to the middle of the office where he stood yesterday, and to speak.

He told us all how shocked he was, and how if any of us needed to take some time off work to process what had happened, then we should speak to HR about it. He also said counselling would be provided if anyone felt in need of it and that was when Jack made a snorting noise which he covered up with a cough. I knew he was trying not to laugh. The strange thing was that I had to clamp my hand over my own mouth, too, because I had an urge to laugh, but I have no idea why.

What Gavin had really come to say, though, was that if any of us were approached by the press then we were to refer them to the Publicity Department. We weren't to give any information out about Evelyn to the press or to talk to them, at all. I don't think that anyone had even thought about speaking to the press until he said it. When he added that it was written into our contracts that we weren't allowed to speak to the media about company business, everyone looked at him in surprise.

It felt like a bit of a threat, which I suppose it was, even coming from very nice Gareth Heath. It made me think that maybe he's not the nice, soft guy that we all took him for and actually, he's probably not that nice because you don't get to be a director by letting people walk all over you, do you?

He finished by saying that from next Monday, Damien Stevens, the current manager from Finance, would be joining us as temporary manager and would run the department until a new person was in place.

Once he'd said his piece he left and there was an uneasy silence hanging over the office. Jackie and Holly, whose desks are closest to mine and Jack's, looked over and pulled faces at us.

'Better keep our gobs shut,' Jackie said, through thickly-painted lips. 'Or else we'll be getting sacked.'

'We should all sell our stories and tell the world what an absolute bitch and a bully she was,' Jack said. 'They can't sack us all.'

'We shouldn't speak ill of the dead,' Jackie said.

''Why not?' Jack said. 'I'm only being honest. I'm not going to pretend I care when I don't. I might ask for counselling to get over the shock of not having to work for a prize bitch anymore.'

We all laughed guiltily and I wondered if anyone would ask for time off; I'd be amazed if someone didn't take advantage of the opportunity to have some paid leave.

'Makes you wonder, though,' Holly said. 'I mean, she must have been vile to other people and not just us, because someone hated her enough to kill her.'

* * *

There are always a group from the office who go to the *Dog and Gun* after work on a Friday for a drink. Sometimes I go, sometimes I don't – and I always drink orange juice. On pay day – or *millionaire's day* as we call it – there's always a good crowd that go but some weeks there'll only be a dozen of the hard-core party animals who like to start early.

Today isn't pay day but everyone apart from

Jackie, who has to get home to see to her old dad, is going.

Me included.

I don't want to go and I'm not a regular but if I don't go it'll look odd, and I don't want anything about me to look odd in any way. I wait my turn at the bar and get myself an orange juice and Jack a pint of lager and take it back to the table. There are so many of us that we've practically commandeered the whole pub and Ian, the landlord, has a smile on his face from ear to ear at the thought of all the money he's going to make.

Darla has already filled him in on the murder of Evelyn and he's looking at us all as if we're having some sort of wake for her, as if somehow, we're raising a glass to her.

We are, but not in the way that he thinks.

I'm sure it won't be long before some tongues are loosened and he'll be getting the lowdown on what Evelyn was really like. There's a bit of a party atmosphere and everyone is also speculating on what our new, temporary boss is going to be like. Everyone has agreed that he can't possibly be as bad as Evelyn and someone, Chrissie, I think, knows someone who works in his existing department and apparently, he's *alright*.

'Why don't you have a proper drink?' Jack asks, as I slide his lager across the table to him. 'I expect you could do with one.'

I can almost taste the vodka and coke on my tongue and it would taste so good right now. I'm so tempted but I can't, because I've promised myself.

'I'm alright with this,' I say, sipping my orange juice.

'You can have one or two,' Jack says, taking several large swallows of his lager. 'I'll make sure you don't go mental and have a binge.'

I fight an internal battle with myself and then I look at the crowd queuing at the bar waiting to be served and the decision is made for me.

'No, I'm just having this and then I'm going home.'

Jack gives me a look that tells me how boring I am and then Darla slides onto the seat next to me and starts talking. She tells us about her wedding and all of the presents they've received and how she's taking a lot of them back because she doesn't like them. I'm relieved to sit here and listen and not have to make conversation. Usually, I find her a bit annoying because she never lets anyone get a word in but right now, I don't want to have to talk so it suits me that she doesn't draw breath.

I sit and listen and sip my juice and eventually excuse myself and go to the toilet, making sure to take my coat and bag with me. When I come back, I don't sit down but stand behind Jack and tap him on the shoulder.

'I'm off, now,' I say.

'Really?' he asks, swivelling around and looking up at me in surprise.

'Yeah, there's a bus in ten minutes and I don't want to miss it.'

A hoot of laughter from Holly draws his attention and he turns to say something and I slip past him and make my way out of the pub, waving at my colleagues as I go with a fixed smile on my face.

I just want to get home and have some peace to think about things.

To think about what I'm going to say if the police ask me what happened when I saw Evelyn.

Because how can I tell them if I can't remember?

CHAPTER SIX

The weekend seemed to last forever and for some reason that I can't fathom, Olivia doesn't seem to be speaking to me. We don't normally have long conversations and truthfully, if she's here I avoid her, but we are usually civil to one another.

When I arrived home on Friday she was already here, which wasn't surprising as I was late after going to the pub. My heart sank when I closed the front door and I could hear her rattling around in the kitchen, because she's extremely hard work and I wasn't in the mood for it. Despite all this I put on my best cheery voice and called out *hello* as I closed the front door.

Silence.

She must have heard me so I didn't call out to her again but I was determined not to let her wind me up. She does this; gives me the silent treatment when I've displeased her in some way. She was in the kitchen in her dressing gown, her face and hair all done, ironing a dress which I assume she was going to wear. So I walked and leaned up against the worktop and attempted to make conversation with her. She never even cracked a smile and instead of her normal aloof indifference and snootiness, I felt distinct animosity from her. I asked her where she was going and tried to be friendly but she answered with muttered one word answers. I eventually gave up and went to my room and stayed there until she'd gone out. Whilst I was waiting for her to leave, I started to get annoyed with myself for even bothering with her; who does she think she is?

I was asleep by the time she came home and I never saw her again until Saturday afternoon and she was exactly the same then except that I didn't bother trying to speak to her, either, so the atmosphere was positively icy. I almost asked her what was wrong and then stopped myself; I don't actually care what her problem is, she could at least be polite. I felt that if I asked her, she would somehow make whatever was bothering her, my fault, so I didn't want to give her the opportunity. Maybe she was still sulking about the washing machine even though she can't prove that it was me. She hasn't asked me for my share of the repair bill and I'm not going to offer it, so if she doesn't speak up I won't be paying it.

She went out again for the evening so at least I had the flat to myself although she did manage to speak just once to tell me that she was having friends over for Sunday lunch, which I'm assuming meant that I shouldn't be here. It did cross my mind to sit in the kitchen and eat a cheese sandwich while they tucked into their Sunday roast but I decided against it. It would make it really uncomfortable for them but I would just look pathetic in the process. I am planning to take the toilet roll and towels out of my bathroom, though.

I thought about staying in my room for the afternoon but I can't face it; I've spent so much time in there lately that I'm beginning to hate it. I really need to get a life and I'm definitely going to just as soon as this Evelyn thing is all over with.

I toyed with the idea of driving down to see my parents because I haven't seen them in over six months, so they're well overdue a visit. They live on the south coast, about an hour-and-a-half away and I really should make the effort but I just can't face it.

The last time I visited, it didn't end well. I stayed for a weekend in February for my brother Nick's 30th birthday party. My parents assumed that I was going to bring Rafe because I hadn't told them that we were over. It was pride, I suppose, and also, I was hoping that we'd get back together again and they'd never need to know that we'd split up. They'd only met Rafe once, even though we were together for over a year, and I'd practically had to twist his arm up his back to make him visit them with me. He didn't *do parents*; he said that he only saw his own once in a blue moon so why did he have to meet mine?

I lured him down there with the promise of a day by the sea and a good meal in an upmarket seafood restaurant but I wish I hadn't bothered. He made absolutely no effort with my parents and he could barely hide his contempt of their semi-detached bungalow on a housing estate where everyone religiously washes their cars and mows the lawn on a Sunday. Mum went into overdrive and got the best china out and bought mountains of cakes from Marks and Spencer. She put on her posh telephone voice and I felt sorry for her and embarrassed by her in equal measure. I wished that I'd never taken Rafe with me. Dad was the complete opposite to Mum and made no secret of the fact that he hated Rafe on sight.

It was awful.

But not as awful as the next visit, when I went alone and made a complete fool of myself at Nick's party. I was wasted, naturally, as Rafe and I were over by then and I'd hit the bottle with a vengeance and spent most of my free time binge-drinking. I can't remember much about the party, which was a good thing but unfortunately, my parents witnessed and remembered every second of it. I spent the next day dying from a hangover with Dad telling me what a disgrace I was. Mum was upset and wanted to know why I'd got so drunk so I lied and said I'd dumped Rafe because he was a cheat. The only good thing to come out of it was that soon afterwards I stopped drinking completely.

Until the day of Rafe's wedding.

We've had telephone conversations since then and we're at the stage now where we don't mention my drunken debacle anymore and are very polite to each other. Even so, I'm not in the mood to face any questioning about my life because yet again, I've stuffed up.

As for my brother – he's still not speaking to me, he says I ruined his party and made him look a joke and he's still trying to live it down.

So what do I do today? Time is ticking by and I know that Olivia's friends will be arriving soon. I need to make a decision or else I'll be stuck here like a lemon while her insufferable friends look at me as if I'm from another planet. As a last resort I start to look online to see what's on at the cinema. A solitary few hours watching a film in the dark is preferable to sitting in my bedroom again. My search is interrupted when my phone bleeps with a message from Jack.

Hiya m8, hows it going?

Not bad, I reply, tho I think Olive's not speaking to me.

That's a good thing, he replies with a laughing face.

My fingers hover over the keys and I wonder if he's on his own or if he has a girl with him. He's always hooking up with some girl or other at weekends – which is another reason why I haven't taken up his offer of sharing his flat. It's no fun sharing with Olivia but do I really want to feel like a permanent third wheel while Jack shags every girl in town? I tap my phone and think; if I knew he was on his own I'd ask if I could go to his place for a few hours to get away from Olivia and her friends.

Come over to mine if you want some olive-free time he texts, as if he's read my mind. *I've just ordered my body weight in pizza and I need you to help me eat it. Also, Fast and Furious is on and it's no fun watching it on my own.*

Will do, I reply, massively relieved that I don't have to sit in a cinema on my lonesome like a complete loser. *I'll bring chocolate,* I add.

Hurry up, he messages, *the pizzas on its way.*

I slip my shoes on, pick my coat and bag up and march down the hallway and let myself out of the front door without bothering to say goodbye to Olivia. I'm not giving her another chance to ignore me.

Luckily, I can walk to Jack's in about twenty minutes so have no need to wait an hour for the Sunday bus that may, or may not, arrive. I'm half-way there when I remember that I forgot to remove the toilet roll and towel from my bathroom.

Shit.

* * *

Jack and I are stretched out on a sofa each, the coffee table between us littered with empty pizza boxes and chocolate wrappers. I'm completely stuffed and couldn't possibly fit in another mouthful even though there's a whole pizza still in its box, untouched.

'Do you think you might have over-ordered a bit, Jack?'

He looks over at me with a puzzled expression.

'What d'ya mean?'

'Well, two of us couldn't eat it all so why did you think you'd manage it all by yourself?'

'It was a deal, buy two get one free and the garlic bread came with it. I couldn't not have it. Wouldn't have made financial sense, would it? It won't be wasted, I'll eat it for breakfast for a few days.'

I laugh and shake my head.

'Cold pizza for breakfast, I don't know how you could eat it, I don't think I could.'

'I'll nuke it in the microwave.'

'Yuk,' I say. 'Even worse.'

'See, this is why you need to move in, you need to civilise me. I need someone to share the rent with but I know if I get another bloke in the place will just turn into a crud-hole and I'll end up lumping him one.'

'Oh, I see,' I say. 'You think you'll get a cleaner as well as a flatmate if I move in, do you?'

'No,' Jack says, looking offended. 'I clean up after myself which is why I don't want another bloke, because I'll end up being the cleaner for him and

I won't be able to stand it. You haven't lived with a man so you don't know what it's like. I'm the exception, not the rule. Most single blokes my age have no idea how to clean; it's as much as they can do to flush a toilet.'

'Sorry,' I say. 'I was only joking.' I was, too. Jack's flat is always immaculate, much better looked after than mine and Olivia's.

'Anyway,' Jack says, opening the pizza box, looking inside and then closing it again. 'Have you decided what you're going to say if the police want to talk to you?'

'Do you think they will?' My heart sinks at the thought of it.

Jack shrugs. 'Who knows? But it's best to be prepared, just in case.'

'I'll just have to tell them the truth,' I say. 'The bits I can remember, anyway.'

'O-k-a-y,' Jack says, drawing the word out slowly.

'Well, I can't deny seeing her, can I? Because if they want to question me it'll be because she's told someone about it or I was seen shouting at her.'

'No,' Jack says. 'You definitely can't deny it.'

'So I'll have to 'fess up; I was off my face on vodka and I can't remember much about it.' I bite my lip. 'It's going to be so embarrassing because word will get out and everyone will know. What if HR decide to issue me with a disciplinary? I wouldn't put it past them because they did it to the guy in planning who slagged off a workmate on Facebook last year. You know how PC they are. They might even sack me.'

I see a vision of the future where I'm sacked and unemployable; a laughing stock who crashed her ex's wedding and behaved like a complete psycho.

'Maybe don't tell them the truth,' Jack says. 'Pretend you do remember. Say that *she* verbally attacked you and you were defending yourself. I mean, it could even be true because you can't remember.'

'But what if she's told someone what happened?'

'It's her word against yours and she's not here to argue about it, is she? If someone saw you, the same thing goes, it's their word against yours.'

'I don't know, it complicates things, lying.'

'We can practice now,' Jack says, swinging his legs down off the sofa and sitting to face me. 'Get your story straight. I'll pretend to be the police and I'll question you, try and trip you up. If they do want to talk to you, then you'll be prepared.'

'What would I say?'

'Say that you went to see her to ask her to stop bullying you. Christ, they've only got to ask anyone in the department what Evelyn was like and they'll back you up. *I'll* back you up. Then the whole company will know what a complete bitch she was.'

I try to imagine lying to the police and keeping that lie going and my stomach churns. Jack is looking at me, an excited expression on his face and I know he's going to be disappointed if I don't take up his idea but I don't think I can do it.

'No,' I say. 'I can't. Lying to the police is a step too far for me. I think it'll be best if I just stick to the truth.'

Jack frowns.

'And I know the potential consequences,' I say. 'And I'll just have to suck it up if it happens. With a bit of luck, she didn't tell anyone and no one saw me and they won't even want to speak to me.'

Jack nods. 'Yep, I see where you're coming from but I don't think you're looking at the whole picture.'

'I am,' I say. 'I'm looking at the worst possible scenario and I'll just have to hope they don't want to question me.'

'No,' Jack says. 'You're not thinking it through properly because what if they think you had something to do with her murder?'

'What?' I laugh. 'I might have been wasted but I never murdered her! I'm a nasty drunk but not a violent one. Well, apart from the odd face slap but that's not real violence, is it?'

'Depends what you call violence,' Jack says. 'The thing is, you can't remember what you did. What if it was more than a slap?'

'I think,' I say, with certainty. 'That I'd remember if I'd murdered someone, no matter how wasted I was.'

Jack stares at me for a moment and then swings his legs back onto the sofa and folds his arms.

'You don't think I'm capable of murder, do you?' I ask.

'Course not,' he says, not looking at me.

'You're not convincing me.'

'Okay,' Jack turns to look at me. 'I'm just going to put this out there and it's not because I think you're a murderer, because of course I don't. But. Sometimes we do things that we don't think we're capable of. A moment of madness, a flip of a switch that can't be undone. Especially when we're drunk.'

'So you think I murdered her?' I almost shout at him.

'No. Maybe, I don't know, I wouldn't blame you, she was such a fucking bitch.'

I gawp at him, unable to believe what I'm hearing.

'Look, the thing that looks weird and that's going to make the police suspicious is that you washed everything you were wearing, didn't you?' Jack says. 'Handbag and everything. If they found out about that it wouldn't look good for you because it's not something you'd normally do when you get home from a night out, is it?'

I stare at him in horror.

No, it's not something I've ever done before.

So why did I do it that night?

CHAPTER SEVEN

It was late when I left Jack's last night; we talked and talked, going around and around in circles until I couldn't think straight. I still haven't decided what I'm going to tell the police if they should question me. I think I was in a state of shock last night; shock that Jack could think me capable of murder and shock that maybe I was the person who killed Evelyn.

Although I'm ninety-nine percent sure that I didn't kill her; I don't think that I'm capable of murder, no matter how much I might hate a person. There's no way I could deliberately kill someone; although the one-percent doubt is there because maybe I pushed her and she fell and knocked her head or something like that. And actually, I didn't even hate Evelyn, I disliked her intensely and I was afraid of what she could do to me and the total control she had over my work-life, but I didn't hate her.

Or maybe I'm fooling myself and I did hate her

a little bit; because didn't I think how convenient it would be if she was accidently knocked over by a bus? And I didn't even feel guilty for thinking it, and I'd have to hate her to wish her dead, wouldn't I?

My head was in a mess so by the time I got home and let myself into the flat I was relieved to see that the place was in darkness, which meant Olivia was already in bed. So I wouldn't have to speak to her or alternatively, ignore her before she ignored me. I went straight through to my bedroom, got undressed and then went back out into the hallway to go to my bathroom, got halfway there and stopped.

Something was different and I had that twitchy feeling you get when something is out of place but you can't quite put your finger on what it is. I looked around but couldn't see what it was that was making me feel that way. The door to Olivia's room was closed, as it usually is, although my bathroom door was wide open, which confirmed that someone had been in there because I closed it before I left to go to Jack's. Thinking I was imagining things, I continued down the hall and was about to go into the bathroom when I realised what it was that was strange; there was a shiny, new, keypad lock fixed to Olivia's door. I stared at it for several minutes trying to make sense of it. Between me going out in the afternoon and coming back that night, Olivia had had a lock fitted on her bedroom door, and I'm guessing that one of the friends she had around for dinner did it for her.

I was a bit shocked because despite what Olivia thinks of me, there's no way that I'd ever go into her bedroom and I thought it was a given that neither of us would go in each other's rooms. I might not like her but I trusted her not to snoop in my room and in my naivety, I expected her to think the same of me. I felt immediately insulted, because why would she have a lock put on her door if it wasn't to stop me from going in there? No one else lives here so it was obviously directed at me. I did think, in that moment, that maybe it was time to take Jack up on his offer of flat-sharing, because why do I want to live with someone who blatantly doesn't trust me?

As I tossed and turned all night, with thoughts of being an unwitting murderer, I wondered what it was about me that made Olivia think I couldn't be trusted. Do I see myself differently to how other people perceive me? Am I, as Rafe so often told me when I accused him of cheating on me, *not right in the head*?

By the time morning came I'd slept for a total of two hours and felt like a washed-out rag. As I hauled myself out of bed and dragged myself down the hallway to the bathroom, the lock on Olivia's door seemed to taunt me and I revised my decision that I'd made during the night to move in with Jack. No, I decided, as I stood under the shower in the hope that I'd feel more awake afterwards, I'm not moving out, because why the hell should I? I've done nothing wrong.

Fuck you, Olivia.

* * *

'He's well lush,' Darla says, as Damien Stevens walks through the department towards Evelyn's old office. He nods and says *good morning* to everyone as he makes his way through the office but he doesn't stop to make conversation with anyone.

'Christ, say it a bit louder, Darl, 'cos I don't think he quite heard you,' Pepe says, furrowing his immaculately shaped eyebrows.

Darla, Pepe, Holly and I are at the mini-kitchen at the end of the office making our pre-work coffee. It's still only quarter-to-nine and we don't start officially until nine o'clock but the majority of the department are already seated at their desks. This is because Evelyn always expected us to begin work the minute we entered the office, no matter how early we arrived. Obviously that rule didn't apply to her; she usually played on her iPad until at least ten o'clock and didn't even try to hide it from us. She mostly left her office door open so she could hear what was going on and she never missed a thing. We often wondered if she had spy cameras set up in the office because there's no way her hearing was so acute she could hear everything from one end of the office to the other. I wonder if our new temporary boss will have the same double standards. The four of us stand and watch as he disappears into Evelyn's old office and I have to agree, he's hot.

'He's alright, though,' Pepe says, quietly. 'And I definitely wouldn't say no.'

'Keep your hands off,' Darla says. 'I saw him first.'

'What? You hussy! You only got married a couple of weeks ago.' Pepe affects to look disgusted and Darla laughs.

'A girl's got to keep a bit of spice in her marriage,' she says, picking up her mug of coffee and walking back to her desk. 'Maybe,' she shouts over her shoulder. 'He swings both ways and then we'll both be happy.' She cackles as she settles herself down in her chair, tosses her head and flicks her scarlet-dyed fringe back out of her eyes. I feel a pang of envy and wish that my life was as open and uncomplicated as hers. Everyone knows that she and *her Darryl* are absolutely besotted with each other and she's all talk and no action about other men. Why can't my life be like that? Why can't my life be normal with a normal boyfriend, why can't I be a regular person and not get myself into such a mess? Why do I have such bad taste in men? Because let's face it, Rafe was the last in a long line of bad choices and I've never managed to learn from my mistakes, always thinking that *this* time it's going to be different.

Why is my whole life such a disaster?

I pour boiling water over the teaspoon of coffee

in my mug and splash some milk in; it looks about as appealing as a cup of mud.

Just about sums up my life.

I trudge back to my desk and get settled and turn my screen on and get ready for the day. Jack isn't in yet, he's made getting into the office with seconds to spare an art form as he refuses to start work one minute earlier than nine o'clock. Bang on one minute to nine, the main door opens and Jack strides in, already unravelling his long scarf and shrugging his jacket off his shoulders as he heads towards his desk. As the hand on the office wall clock reaches the hour, he's seated in his swivel chair and his screen is on. I don't know how he does it.

'Is the new bloke in already?' he asks quietly, staring pointedly at Evelyn's office door which is now firmly closed.

'He is,' I say. 'Maybe he'll come out and introduce himself. He did say good morning as he went by.'

'Wow, that was big of him,' Jack snorts.

Seconds later the door opens and Damien Stevens appears and stands in the doorway looking around the office. I see the surprised look on Jack's face because Damien is indeed, very hot and not the old duffer we were expecting. Tall, dark and handsome, he's young, too, in his mid to late thirties. We'd all assumed that whoever took over from Evelyn would be a dusty old manager who was looking for a peaceful billet to see out his remaining days in the company before drawing his pension. Maybe that's who we'll eventually end up with as Damien is only temporary, although temporary in this company has been known to last ten years.

'Hi everyone,' Damien says, walking casually into the middle of the office. He gives me and Jack a warm smile as he passes by and comes to a stop at the centre of the office.

'I don't know about everyone else,' he says, as he looks around. 'But I like to start the week with a decent cup of coffee on a Monday morning so how about you all join me in the staff restaurant? I'll treat you all to a Starbucks and we can get to know a little about each other.'

He doesn't have to ask twice; a Starbucks beats an instant coffee made in the office any day of the week and people are practically jumping up from their seats in their haste to get to the door. Jack and I fall in behind the mass exodus as we trail out of the office.

'I'm going to have their special, with extra cream and sprinkles, and maybe a Danish, too,' Jack says, as we climb the stairs to the staff restaurant.

'Take full advantage, then, Jack,' I say, with a laugh.

'Too fucking right,' he mutters. 'He'll be claiming it all back on expenses, anyway.'

'He will,' I say. 'But it's still more than Evelyn ever did. She never bought us so much as a sweet, even at Christmas, even though she used to get a massive bonus and a personal present from Gareth Heath.'

Jack grunts a reply and we fall in behind everyone else and all thirty-eight of us troop into the restaurant and head for the Starbucks counter. Brenda, the server behind the counter, looks as if she's going to have a panic attack when she sees us all and reinforcements are soon drafted in from the breakfast counter to help. We give our orders and Brenda writes them down on a paper napkin and I wonder if any of us will end up with the right drink. Brenda has trouble with more than three customers waiting so I don't think the odds are good. We mill around and find somewhere to sit in the large coffee lounge area which is often used for staff meetings.

Damian positions himself on a padded stool in the centre of our throng and we all await our drinks. Unlike Evelyn, Damien is easy to talk to with a casual and easy-going manner. Everyone has to introduce themselves and say what their job is – most of us do basically the same job, marketing stats – so the introductions don't take very long. Damien tells us he's come from Finance, which we already knew, and his deputy has currently stepped into his old role. He doesn't tell us how long he's staying and when Jackie asks, he side-steps the question and says that he's not sure. We do have a serious bit where he says how sad it is that Evelyn died, and everyone does their duty and looks mournful, except for Jack, who sniffs and looks bored, but it doesn't last very long and we're soon back to talking about work and the company.

By the time Damien has finished his pep talk, Jack, Chrissie and I are still waiting for our coffees and we stay in the coffee lounge while Damien and the others head back to the office. As they leave, Damien asks me if I can pop into his office when I've finished my coffee to discuss my project with him. I look at him blankly for a moment before realising that he means the special task that Evelyn set for me. I can't help feeling impressed that he remembered my name.

Five minutes after the rest of the office have left, Chrissie's coffee arrives and she scuttles back to the office, leaving Jack and I still waiting.

'Might have known we'd be last,' I say, with a sigh.

'Suits me,' Jack says, putting his feet up on the chair in front of him. 'Less time in the office.'

'True,' I say. 'He seems okay though, doesn't he? Much nicer than Evelyn.'

'Christ, you're a pushover,' Jack says with a frown. 'He's a wanker just like the rest of them.'

'He might not be,' I say, having no idea why I'm defending him.

Jack snorts. 'Teacher's pet. Just because you have a *project.*'

I'm saved from answering by the arrival of our coffees and Jack's Danish and I sip my drink while he tucks into his pastry.

'Want a bite?' he asks, while ramming most of it

into his mouth.

'No, you're alright,' I say, with a smile.

I sit and drink my coffee and hope that Jack's wrong, that Damien is going to be a decent boss.

Surely we can't be so unlucky to get another one like Evelyn.

* * *

I think Jack is wrong; I think that Damien's going to be fine. I was a bit nervous when I went in to see him about my *project*, but unlike Evelyn, he didn't make any veiled threats about what would happen if I made any mistakes. He seemed keen to impress on me that it was a learning curve and as such, mistakes were to be expected. He made being given a project sound like a reward, not the first step towards dismissal. He was easy to talk to, too, and seemed genuinely interested in how long I'd worked for the company and where I'd worked before.

Totally different to Evelyn.

When I came back out Jack barely spoke to me and he seemed in a funny mood all day, and I wondered if it was because I still haven't decided what I'm going to say to the police if they do question me. Jack's a really good mate but I've noticed that he does get a bit huffy if I don't take his advice. He's not alone; whenever a man gives advice they expect it to be taken. Or it could be nothing to do with that, maybe it's because now that we have a stand-in for Evelyn, Damien is going to cramp Jack's style. Last week Jack disappeared every day for hours at a time and was pretty much coming and going as he pleased and now he won't be able to do that anymore. He'd swan off and if anyone asked, which they mostly didn't, he'd say he had a dentist or doctor's appointment, even though I know that he was going home to put his feet up or going shopping. He asked if I wanted to go with him but I said no because even though it's nice to be free of Evelyn, I do actually like my job and I do have a bit of pride in it.

At lunchtime I did a bit of internet searching about Evelyn's murder and there was nothing more in the online newspaper than there was the other day. I don't know if that's a good or bad thing. Maybe it was a random murder and she was in the wrong place at the wrong time, or someone broke into her house and it was a burglary gone wrong. Maybe she had a secret boyfriend or girlfriend that none of us knew about and they'd had a gutful of her because if she was anything like she was at work, she'd be totally hateful. I don't know, because like I say, the police don't seem to be giving any details. Maybe no news is good news and the police don't know about my run in with her.

Fingers crossed.

By the time five o'clock came around I still hadn't decided what to do about the police if they should want to question me but I had made a decision about one thing: the bin bag with the clothes in that I wore on Saturday, has to go. Luckily, it's bin day tomorrow for our block of flats so I'm going to take the bag down to the communal dustbins and stuff it into one of them. I intended doing this anyway so it's not as if I'm doing it because I have anything to hide, is it? If there's any possibility that I'm a suspect, why make the police more suspicious by having a bag of wet clothing that I wore in the bottom of my wardrobe? I definitely don't want any of it because I'll never wear that white dress again knowing the reason why I bought it.

With a muttered *bye*, Jack has his jacket on and is gone before I've even had a chance to close my screen down. I have the distinct feeling that I've pissed him off and I wonder why it is that men are so moody and behave like spoilt brats just because you don't take their advice. I decide to walk home instead of catching the bus, even though it takes a good thirty minutes, because although it's cold it's a dry and pleasant evening. I've been hunched over a desk all day and I need to stretch my legs and feel as if I've actually done some form of exercise.

When I get home, I let myself into the flat and Evelyn isn't in, which is an absolute bonus. Hopefully she's gone straight out from work and won't be home until late, by which time I'll be in bed. I need to get over the annoyance of the lock on her door so it's better that I don't see her for a while. If I see her, I might just have a go at her and I don't really want to fall out with her because then I'll *have* to move out. Jack's moodiness today has reminded me that he's not happy all the time – who is? – but I don't really want to move in with him and put up with his sulking every time I don't do what he says.

I don't take my coat off but go straight into my bedroom to get the bin bag so I can take it down to the bins. If I take my coat off and sit down, I'll forget all about it and miss bin day tomorrow. Maybe I'll empty the swing bin in the kitchen, too, to show Olivia that I am a capable adult and not a complete waste of space. I pull open the wardrobe door but can't see the bin bag so I pull open the other door but it's not there either. Maybe I buried it underneath the pile of shoes in there, because it's not exactly tidy and all of the shoes are tossed in a heap on top of each other.

Ten minutes later I've taken everything out of the bottom of the wardrobe and put it all back again and I have to face the truth.

The bag is gone.

CHAPTER EIGHT

When I couldn't find the bag in the wardrobe, at first I refused to believe that it was gone and I turned the whole room upside down but it was pointless, the bin bag was not anywhere in that room.

I sat on the floor shoving everything back underneath my bed that I'd pulled out and tried to think. Did I put the bag in the communal dustbin on Sunday? I know that I thought about doing it, so did I take it down there and I've forgotten, because I *was* massively hungover and not thinking properly. I remember telling myself that I'd leave going down to the communal bins until another day when I didn't feel so ill, because I couldn't even keep sips of water down and spent most of the day with my head hanging over the toilet.

But I must have taken it down there, because it's not in my bedroom and there's nowhere else it could be.

The only person who could have taken the bag from my room is Olivia – and why would she take a bag of wet clothing? She wouldn't; which means that I not only suffer blackouts when I drink, I'm not even aware of what I'm doing the day *after* a massive binge, when I'm sober.

What a mess.

That awful weekend of Rafe's wedding has been a turning-point for me.

It's time to move on and grow up.

Yes, he treated me badly, but I'm not the first woman to be dumped or cheated on and it's not as if it's even the first time that it's happened to me.

I need to get over Rafe.

I think, actually, that I am over him and have been for a while. The whole crashing the wedding thing was about letting Rafe know that it wasn't okay to treat me like that. It was meant to be some sort of revenge when in reality, all I did was humiliate myself. Again. Because I should have ditched him the minute I knew he was cheating on me, instead of allowing him to treat me like shit. He used me and treated me like I didn't matter and I allowed him to do that because deep down, I thought he was too good for me.

I thought I was lucky to have him.

But I now know that he was never mine; I was useful, someone to have sex with and pass the time with until someone more suitable came along. I think that underneath my longing and love for him, I always knew that. I should have been dignified and walked away with my head held high instead of chasing and hounding him, getting smashed and professing undying love for him while his jeering, posh friends looked on in unconcealed amusement.

I cringe now at my behaviour and I wish I could undo the events of not only that Saturday, but for most of the time that I was with him.

But I can't change the past, I have to move on.

Time to grow up, Josie, at the grand old age of twenty-eight.

* * *

Despite the events of that Saturday hanging over my head, I've actually enjoyed coming to work since Evelyn's been gone. The cloud of nastiness that pervaded the office is no more and I no longer feel that I have to triple check everything I do to make sure I haven't made any mistakes. I know that it's only Wednesday and Damien's been here for a total of three days but the atmosphere is unbelievably different.

He's called me into his office several times to talk him through my project, because as he says, he's finance and not marketing so it's all quite new to him. He's very easy to talk to and not like a boss at all, and we've chatted about things other than work and it feels quite normal and natural. Everyone in the office agrees that we've hit lucky with him and we hope that he stays for a while.

We definitely don't want to end up with another Evelyn. Jack doesn't agree about Damien; he says we're all pushovers for a pretty face and a bit of charm and that Damien will soon show his true colours. I hope he's wrong, because Evelyn has to be the exception for her nastiness and not every boss has to be like her.

Actually, Jack is being a bit of an arse. He's still in a right grump and the only time he's spoken to me since Monday is to moan about something. Everything I say to him is met with a sneer or a grumble and I've now decided to keep my mouth shut. He has these weird moods now and I'm not going to ask him what's wrong because he won't tell me anyway. If I ask, he'll just say *he's fine*, in a completely un-fine way. I know from experience that he'll suddenly snap out of it and be okay again and I'll never know what it was all about.

Because he's in such a mood I haven't told him that I can't find the bag of clothes and maybe that's not a bad thing because I'm trying very hard not to obsess over it. If I tell him we'll just end up talking about it endlessly and there's no point because it doesn't achieve anything. Besides, do I really want to admit that I have no idea what I did with it?
No, I don't; I don't want to admit that not only do I get so pissed that I can't remember what I've done, I can't remember the next day either.

Despite the clothes thing and Jack's mood, I'm feeling more positive this week and I'm hopeful that the police know nothing of my argument with Evelyn. It's nearly two weeks since she was murdered and I'm sure if the police knew about me they'd have questioned me by now. I've even been thinking that I should look into furthering my career here because that's what I intended when I took the job. I've never applied for any of the opportunities that pop up every week but have been content to sit here in Marketing for the last three years out of sheer laziness. This is a large company and who knows what I could achieve if I put my mind to it.

I think I need to try a bit harder with Olivia, too. We're never going to be friends and I don't like her but there's no reason we can't be civil to each other. The rent I pay her is very reasonable and the location is ideal, I'm in the centre of town and I can walk to work if I need to. Perhaps I should do that more often, instead of getting the bus. The exercise would do me good and it would save me money. My aim is to buy my own place and at the moment I'm easily able to save a lot of my wages for the deposit. If I hadn't been so bloody stupid over Rafe I'd be in my own flat by now. I practically forced him to let me move in with him when I lied and told him that my landlord was selling up and I had nowhere to live. He wasn't keen and said I could stay for a while but my plan was that once I'd moved in, he'd realise that we were perfect for each other and we'd have a happy ever after. It didn't work, all that happened was that I gave up my own rented flat and spent all of my savings trying to buy his love with expensive gifts and meals at fancy restaurants, even though he had far more money than me.

Lesson learned.

I could move in with Jack and still save up because he's only asking for the same amount of rent as I pay Olivia. But do I really want to live with a good mate and risk our friendship? I love Jack to bits but his moods are annoying and also, with all the girls he has staying over on weekends, I could end up feeling like a spare part. And what if I get a new boyfriend? I'm going to feel awkward inviting him over with Jack there, there's something about having a male flatmate that's not quite the same as another woman.

I really need to get over my beef about Olivia putting a lock on her door. I've taken it personally but maybe she's a nervous sleeper, maybe she has a fear of someone breaking in at night. She's a completely different personality to me, she could be a nervous wreck for all I know because I've made no effort to get to know her properly. Her aloofness could be nervousness, for all I know. Maybe, the next time I see her I should just ask her why she's had a lock put on her door and stop assuming that it's all about me. I haven't seen her since Sunday, but I know she's been at the flat because her washing up has been left on the drainer. She must be coming home late and leaving early in the morning. Actually, in many ways, she's the ideal flatmate because she's hardly ever at home.

I check the office clock; twelve-thirty, time for lunch. I walk down the office and take my lunchbox out of the fridge and take it back to my desk. I made myself cheese sandwiches this morning, how good am I? Proper grown up and it'll save me buying an expensive sandwich from the staff restaurant. I open the lunchbox, take out my sandwich and take a huge bite and flick my screen over to the internet. I click on the local newspaper to see that there's not much in the way of news. I scroll down the page and see that there's a news item with a picture of Evelyn. I click on it with a feeling of dread. I feel a huge weight lifting as I read that a local man, age 49, is helping the police with their enquiries.

I feel my face break out into a smile and then compose myself, I don't want anyone asking me what I'm smiling about but inside I'm jumping around doing somersaults.

It seems I'm off the hook.

* * *

At half-past four, Katie, the HR manager, clomps down the office in her skyscraper heels and sashays past mine and Jack's desk and into Damien's office. She closes the door behind her and leaves a waft of cloying perfume in her wake. Damien must be suffocating in there.

Katie is known as a bit of a man-eater and

has worked her way through quite a few of the younger managers even though she's well past forty herself. Jack reckons she's nearer fifty than forty and her face is starting to look slightly weird with all of the fillers and Botox she's had but there's no denying she has a stunning, curvaceous figure.

I wonder if she's come to tell Damien that they've found a replacement for Evelyn's job already and the thought of it makes me feel disappointed. But that's unlikely because it usually takes months to recruit someone, even from inside the company.

Maybe they've charged someone with Evelyn's murder.

The thought pops into my mind and refuses to budge; the online newspaper said that a man was helping the police with their enquiries – isn't that what they say when the police have a suspect but haven't yet charged anyone?

I think it is.

The door opens and Katie struts out, chest thrust forward, followed by Damien, who looks very grim-faced. He follows Katie to the centre of the office where he coughs to get everyone's attention, although he already has it because no one misses a thing in here. Katie stands right next to him, giving him a full view of her ample cleavage which is straining the buttons of her silk blouse.

'Everyone,' he says. 'If I could just have your

attention for a moment? So,' he says, looking around at everyone. 'Katie has just been contacted by the police investigating Evelyn's murder.'

I hold my breath and wait but I can't help the feeling of relief that starts to build in me, this is it; this is the end of an anxious two weeks and my life can go back to normal. But a better life than my old one, because I'm definitely turning over a new leaf. It crosses my mind that Evelyn could have had a boyfriend and that's who the police are questioning. We all knew that she lived alone but that doesn't mean that she wasn't seeing someone.

'And to make it easier for everyone, Katie has asked, and I've agreed, that the team can come in on Friday and conduct their questioning in the meeting room.'

I glance over at Jack, who's looking as confused as I am.

'Sorry,' Damien says, seeing the puzzled looks from my colleagues. 'I'm not making myself clear. The police want to question everyone in the office and they're coming in on Friday morning.'

There's a buzz around the office and Damien holds his hand up.

'They're going to interview everyone starting at nine-thirty and it may possibly go on into next week, as there are a lot of you. Any questions?'

I have a question, but it's not one that I can ask Damien.

What the hell am I going to say to the police?

CHAPTER NINE

Friday finally arrives and I'm awake at four o'clock; just as I was yesterday. Ever since Damien announced that the police were coming today, I've been in a constant state of anxiety. I still haven't made a decision as to what I'm going to say to them and the same questions keep churning around in my head as if my brain is a demented washing machine.

Why are they questioning everyone in the office?

Are we all suspects or is it just me that they're after and they're trying to hide that fact?

Why are they bothering questioning us if a man is helping with their enquiries?

The police visit has a been a hot topic of conversation in the office since Wednesday and the general consensus seems to be that they're checking to find out if anyone knows something about Evelyn's private life that they don't already know. But I can't help wondering why they're waited until now to question us. It's over two weeks ago since she was murdered; or maybe two weeks isn't long in a police investigation. Maybe I've watched too many police dramas where everything happens in the space of a few hours.

What if they ask when I last saw Evelyn, do I lie or do I tell the truth? As soon as I make the decision to do one thing, I immediately talk myself out of it and decide on the opposite. I then repeat the process endlessly.

I need to talk to Jack about it but he wasn't in work yesterday; he rang in sick and because he's been in such a mood for the last few days, I felt as if I couldn't ring him and talk to him. We'd probably just talk around in circles anyway but I feel very alone and a bit pissed off with him to be honest. He's supposed to be my best mate and because of his moods I can't even talk to him about how I feel.

I drag myself out of bed and pad along to the bathroom and throw myself into the shower and stand underneath the hot water as if it will make me feel better. I have to treat this day just like any other; I've committed no crime, apart from getting blind drunk, and I need to keep that thought firmly in my mind. I get dressed and make a special effort with my hair and makeup to make myself feel better. I tell myself that it's not for Damien's benefit, even though I have a sneaking suspicion that it might be. Not that there's any way he'd even look at me but a girl can dream, can't she?

I walk into the kitchen, fully ready for work and

it's only a quarter-to-eight. I'm surprised to see Olivia seated at the table drinking a cup of coffee, but what's even more surprising is that she's wearing a cream towelling dressing gown. I don't think I've ever seen her not looking immaculately dressed and as if she's just stepped off the pages of a fashion magazine. She looks weird; like when you see people without glasses when they normally wear them.

'Hi, Olivia,' I say, with a smile, remembering my new resolution to be pleasant and behave like a grown up. 'How are you? We're like ships that pass in the night, lately, aren't we?'

She doesn't answer me but stands up and pulls the belt of her dressing gown more tightly and folds her arms and looks down at her feet.

'I need to talk to you, Josephine,' she says, to the floor.

'Okay, I'm all ears,' I say, as pleasantly as I can despite the annoyance I feel at her using my full name. She doesn't make it easy to be nice to her but I'll do my best. No doubt I'm going to get a telling off for leaving the remote control on the sofa or something equally trivial.

'The thing is,' she says, finally managing to look in the general direction of my face. 'I'm going to have to give you notice to move out.'

I stare at her and imagine having to move in with Jack, who's barely speaking to me, and I realise that I really, really don't want to move out.

'But why?' I ask. 'I thought we got along fine. I

mean, we rarely see each other but when we do we're okay, aren't we?' A bit of a lie, but I don't want to just agree with her.

'Well, it's a bit awkward,' Olivia says, in her aloof, snooty way, still avoiding eye-contact with me. 'So maybe it's best if we leave the reasons why and just agree a date for your leaving?'

'I don't think so,' I say. 'If you're throwing me out then I think I have a right to know why.' Olivia flinches when I speak and I think I might have been a bit forceful in the way I spoke. Sod it, if she's chucking me out she can at least have the guts to give me a reason.

'Alright,' she says, with a sigh. 'If you insist.' She picks her cup up from the table and walks over to the sink and puts the cup on the draining board and turns to face me. She takes a deep breath and the words tumble out in a rush. 'You've been going into my room and taking my things and moving stuff around. You might have noticed that I've had a lock put on the door but I've decided that I'm not comfortable with what you're capable of and I'd like you to leave.'

It's not as if it's a shock, her thinking I've been in her room, I was expecting her to say that.

The shock is that when she said it, she looked scared.

Of me.

* * *

There's an air of excitement in the office and gossip is buzzing around in the air like a swarm of bees. I arrive early, at twenty-to-nine, but apart from Jack, I'm the last person in. It's noticeable that everyone seems to have made a special effort with their appearance today as if an interview with the police is a special occasion.

I hang my coat up and get my work out for the day but don't bother to make myself a coffee. I can't stomach it. There's no sign of Jack, and that's no surprise because if he is coming in, he'll arrive with a minute to spare as he usually does. As I log in on my PC I run Olivia's words over in my head again. She refused to elaborate on what I was supposed to have taken from her bedroom or why she thought I'd been in there, but just kept repeating that she hoped I wasn't going to *make things difficult*.

I've decided that I'm not going to put up a fight because I don't want to live with someone who's obviously afraid of me. I think that Olivia is having some sort of breakdown and is projecting her anxieties onto me. I'd always assumed that her rigidity and coldness were just a part of her general snootiness, but now I'm thinking that she's actually a nervous wreck and that's her way of coping. The sooner I move out, the better.

Which means that Jack needs to get out of his mood so I can move in to his as soon as possible. Staying at his will give me some breathing space to find the right room to rent where I can continue saving for a deposit on my own place. Jack's recent black mood has confirmed that it's not a good idea to flat share with him on a long-term basis, although obviously I won't tell him that. I'll let him assume that I'm staying permanently and put up with his sulking when I find somewhere else to live and move out. A bit underhand, I grant you, but I have to do what's right for me and hopefully, if he's a true friend, he'll understand. And anyway, he might quickly get fed up with having me living with him because I'm not perfect, either. He's a neat freak and whilst I'm not massively untidy, I'm a long way from his high standards.

Jack slides behind his desk at a minute to nine and I look over and say *hello*. I can tell by his face and the way he answers that he's still in a mood and a cloud of depression settles over me. For fuck's sake, Jack, I can do without you sulking. Something or someone has pissed him off but I'll never know who, or why, or if it's me because he never says. Like all men when they get a gob on, it's all a big mystery that they can't possibly talk about. I just can't be bothered to pander to him today. Out of courtesy I ask him if he's feeling better after his day off sick and he mutters that *he's fine*. I don't bother after that. Get on with it, Jack, and while you're about it, fucking grow-up.

At ten-past-nine there's a flurry of excitement as a man and a woman enter the office. They're both dressed in suits but we all know that they're the police officers who've come to interview us.

Katie from HR is behind them and she steers them straight by the desks at the bottom of the office and into the meeting room and swiftly closes the door. I'm sure I can smell her perfume from all the way down the office and I wonder why she thinks it appropriate to wear a skin-tight mini-dress to work.

'Fuck me,' Jack says, quietly. 'What a fucking dog.'

I look up in surprise. The cold expression has gone from his face and happy-go-lucky normal Jack is back and he's grinning.

I laugh, although I don't find him funny. Yes, Katie is dressed totally inappropriately for work but I don't like to hear a man talk about another woman that way. I feel relieved that he's out of his mood so I'm not going to tackle him on his comment now and put him straight back into a sulk. I'm surprised at how quickly he's changed. And also, if I'm honest, a little annoyed, but I won't show it because right now I need all the friends I can get.

'I wonder who's going to be first in?' Jack asks.

'Maybe they'll do it alphabetically, or start at that end of the office and work their way up, which means we'll be last.'

All I hope is that I'm not first because I want to have some idea of what questions the police are going to ask. The meeting room door opens and Katie clip clops out looking very pleased with herself. She struts up the office towards us and I think that's it, I'm first, but she stops when she reaches Pepe and speaks to him and he stands up and follows her back to the meeting room. He looks nervous and I think that's a good thing, because being interviewed by the police makes people feel nervous even when they're perfectly innocent. He goes into the meeting room and closes the door and Katie walks back across the office and leaves by the main door without speaking to anyone else.

Jack looks at Damien's closed door and then looks at me meaningfully.

'Have you decided what you're going to say?' he whispers.

I sigh.

'No idea,' I say. 'I've spent the night tossing and turning and changing my mind every five minutes and if that wasn't bad enough, I got up this morning and Olivia wants me to move out.'

'What?' Jack says. 'Why?'

I shrug.

'Who knows,' I lie. 'Something about wanting the place to herself and not needing a flatmate anymore.'

'Bloody cheek,' Jack says. 'Doesn't matter now, though, 'cos I need a flatmate and you can move into mine as soon as you like.'

'Thanks, mate,' I say, with a smile, and then wonder why I'm lying to him. He's known me long enough to know that I'm not capable of stealing or snooping in Olivia's room, so why don't I just tell him? I know he'd agree that Olivia's having some sort of mental health crisis, so why am I keeping it a secret?

Because, for some reason, I feel ashamed that someone would even think me a thief, as if someone thinking it makes it a possibility. Also, Jack didn't seem to think that me murdering Evelyn was completely unbelievable and that's much worse than stealing, so what does that say about me?

'The room's all ready,' he says. 'Whenever you want to move in.'

'Thanks,' I say.

'Hey up,' Jack says, looking down the office towards the meeting room. 'Pepe's out.'

'Christ, that was quick, can't have been more than ten minutes.'

'They can't be asking very many questions,' Jack says, as Pepe walks down the office towards us.

'No, they can't.' I agree.

Which is just as well, because Pepe stops in front of my desk.

'You're next up, Josie,' he says, with a laugh. 'Time to confess your sins.'

CHAPTER TEN

As I walk down the office towards the meeting room, I can hear Pepe speaking behind me and Jack laughing and I experience a weird out of body experience. For a moment I feel as if I'm not here and am watching someone else walk towards something they dread.

Dead woman walking.

In the few minutes of that walk, I give myself a good talking to. I've committed no crime, I keep reminding myself, I'm not a murderer or a thief. But it doesn't work and by the time I enter the meeting room I'm just about ready to offer my wrists up so they can slap the handcuffs on straight away and get it over with.

'Hi,' the policewoman says, looking up at me with a smile. 'Josephine Burrows?'

'Yes,' I say. 'Josie.'

'Please, take a seat, Josie.' She waves her hand across the table and I sit down in the chair opposite them both.

'Hi, Josie.' It's the man speaking now, he also smiles. 'I'm Detective Sergeant Rossiter and this is Detective Constable Cairns.'

I nod at them both and give them a tip-lipped, mouth closed smile.

'So,' DS Rossiter says. 'We just have a few questions to ask you to assist with our investigation into Ms Pemberton's death, shouldn't take too long. Is that okay?'

No, I want to scream, *it's not okay*, but I keep my face impassive while I wait for them to get on with it.

'I know that her death has been a tremendous shock to you all and any help that you can give us will be most appreciated,' he adds.

'Have you caught who did it?' I ask, because wouldn't everyone ask this? It's a perfectly normal question.

'I'm sorry,' DS Rossiter says, with a condescending smile. 'We're unable to discuss the investigation with you. I'm sure you understand.'

'Of course,' I say. I wonder if they've charged the man who's helping them with their enquiries.

'Miss Burrows,' DC Cairns says, with a smile that never reaches her eyes. 'You've worked here...' She pauses and taps some keys on the keyboard in front of her. 'Three years, is that right?'

'Yes, that's right,' I say. 'Three years last October.'

'And you've worked for Ms Pemberton for all of that time?'

'Yes,' I say.

'And how well would you say you knew Ms Pemberton?'

I pause and think before answering.

'Not at all in a personal sense,' I say. 'Even though I've worked here for three years, it was strictly a working relationship so the only contact I had with Evelyn, Ms Pemberton, was about work.'

DC Cairns nods, her business-like pony-tail bobbing efficiently as she taps at the keys on her laptop. I guess that this is what Pepe told her as well. She'll get the same answer from everyone in the department because none of us were friends with Evelyn. She'd occasionally come out of her office and park herself by random desks to brag about her recent purchases, especially around bonus time, or about the luxury holidays she'd booked, but it was strictly one way as she wasn't remotely interested in anyone else's life.

But would Pepe have said that I was Evelyn's latest victim, is that why I've been called in so soon? My stomach cramps in anxiety. I clench my stomach muscles and force myself not to look away from DC Cairns in case it makes me look guilty.

DC Cairns finishes typing and looks up and gives me her cold smile again.

'So you don't know anything about Ms Pemberton's private life?' she asks.

'No, nothing.'

She starts typing again and I feel myself relax as I realise that I've been called in after Pepe because my surname begins with a B and Pepe's begins with an A. They're calling us in alphabetically. They're asking about her private life because they already have a suspect and they need to know if any of us knew about him.

'She never mentioned anything about her personal life at all?' DC Cairns asks, continuing to type.

'Nothing.' I shake my head.

'Okay, I think that's all we need,' DS Rossiter says, obviously feeling a bit left out. 'Thank you for your help.'

'No problem,' I say, standing up and trying to stop the relief from showing on my face.

'Could you ask Susan Cheeseman to come in next, please?'

'Of course,' I say. 'No problem.'

I'm almost at the door when DC Cairns voice stops me.

'Oh, sorry, one more thing, Miss Burrows. Could you tell us the last time that you saw Ms Pemberton?'

* * *

I lied.

I told them that the last time I saw Evelyn was when I left work on Friday evening. DC Cairns typed my reply on her laptop and DS Rossiter barely looked at me as he was too busy picking at his nails. I'm sure it was a standard question that they ask everyone and they have no idea about me seeing her on Saturday.

Almost sure.

It's done now, anyway, and I can hardly go back and tell them the truth, can I? And just the thought of sitting in that room and telling them about what I did on that day is more than I can bear. I've lied now and if they find out, I'll just have to take the consequences of lying to the police. If they do find out, maybe I'll just pretend that I can't remember seeing her. I was so wasted, it's quite possible. A man is helping them with their enquiries so it's only a matter of time before he's charged and they're questioning everyone to find out if we know who he is. Maybe Evelyn treated him as badly as she treated us.

But my face flushed when they asked and they must have noticed. Would they see that as a sign that I was lying?

All of these thoughts rush through my head as, on autopilot, I walk to Susan's desk and tell her that she's next. Her face flushes and she picks up her handbag and then puts it down again.

'Why would I need my handbag?' She laughs, as she stands up.

'Well, you never know,' I say.

'What do they want to know?' she whispers, as I start to walk away.

'Not much,' I say. 'Just if you knew anything about her private life. Nothing to worry about.'

'I don't know why,' she says. 'But as soon as I see

a policeman, I feel guilty!'

'I know,' I say. 'I'm the same. Honestly, Susie, they're really nice, no need to worry.'

She smiles and heads towards the meeting room. Susie's a bag of nerves most of the time anyway, she used to jump a mile if Evelyn went anywhere near her desk. If I looked guilty in there, God knows what Susie will look like.

On the way back to my desk, three people stop me to find out what the police ask and whether they've been forthcoming about having caught anyone. There's disappointment that I don't have any juicy gossip and I can feel that the air of excitement in the office first thing this morning is rapidly diminishing.

Damien is standing talking to Jack as I reach my desk and he turns and says *good morning* with a smile and I feel my face flush again. For God's sake, I'm turning into a teenager again. I slide into my seat and concentrate on my screen and pretend to start work.

'Alright, mate?'

I look up to see that Damien has gone and Jack is looking at me expectantly.

'Well?' he asks.

'All good,' I say.

He raises an eyebrow and I glance quickly around to make sure no one is looking or listening.

'I lied,' I mouth, silently.

'Good girl,' Jack says, a big grin breaking out over his face.

I grin back but inside I'm annoyed.

Why is it so important that I take his advice? Why does he have to be right all the time?

Typical man.

* * *

The whole office, Damien included, go to the *Dog and Gun* after work. Jack pulls a face when he finds out that Darla had invited Damien because he says he'll cramp our style. I tell him that with thirty-eight of us we don't have to be anywhere near him but Jack scowls and mutters *that bosses should know when to fuck off*. I think Jack's put out because there's another man in the office. Out of the thirty-eight of us there are only eight men and Jack was the most eligible and attractive out of all of them before Damien arrived and now, he's not. Not that Jack would ever admit that Damien is better looking than him.

I don't always bother to go to the pub but it would look odd if I was the only one not going because everyone wants to talk about the police visit.

Not that there's much to talk about; it's quite clear that the police have asked everyone the same questions and given absolutely nothing away about the investigation.

I stick to orange juice and after an hour-and-a-half I've had enough of listening to the same things being repeated over and over by different people but I'm loath to go home. The thought of being greeted by Olivia with her frightened eyes isn't appealing.

'Christ, this is a bore-off,' Jack says, coming over and standing next to me.

'I know,' I say. 'I'm probably going to head back to mine, soon, though I can't say I feel exactly welcome there.'

'Come back to mine,' Jack says. 'We can order take-out and watch some telly. You can have a look at your room, see if there's anything you want to change in there before you move in.'

'Really?' I ask. 'You're not going out or anything?'

'Nah, can't be arsed tonight.'

'Thanks, then, I will.'

We finish our drinks and after a few goodbyes to those nearest, we make our way out of the pub and head towards Jack's place. It's raining, of course, but we decide that it'll take longer to wait for a bus than it will to walk so we march briskly along.

When we arrive at Jack's we go into the lounge and I hang my coat over a dining chair near the radiator to dry and look properly at the place with flat share eyes. It's a nice flat, with big rooms; it's nicer than Olivia's actually. The furniture is new and pristine although the place lacks character; there are no squashy cushions or knick-knacks to make it feel more homely, it lacks a woman's touch. As I look around, I can't stop my eyes from straying to the double doors that open onto the balcony.

Just the thought of stepping outside and looking over the railing is enough to start me hyper-ventilating.

'Don't worry, they're locked,' Jacks says, watching me.

'It's irrational, I know, but balconies make me nervous. It's all very well being six floors up but I can forget about it when I'm inside; outside is another matter.'

'You don't need to worry,' Jack says. 'It's always locked. The only time I open it is to go out for a fag and I always close it behind me to keep the smoke out.'

I laugh, although when he's not looking I'll be checking the key to make sure it really *is* locked.

'Anyway, do you want to see your room?' Jack asks.

'Please,' I say.

I follow him back out into the hallway and he opens the bedroom door with a flourish. It's a large room with a double bed in the middle which is made up with a pink duvet set. There's a wardrobe on one wall and a chest of drawers positioned underneath the window. The furniture looks new and the walls are painted in an off-white colour and it all looks very fresh. I'm thrilled to see that this room has an ensuite; no one else will be using it except for me.

'It's lovely, Jack. I love the pink duvet set, did it belong to your old flatmate?'

'No.' Jack laughs. 'That's an old one my mum

gave me, I made the bed up 'cos I don't like rooms that look unlived in.'

I walk around the room, admiring it, trailing my hand over the bed. 'Wow, Jack,' I say. 'It all looks so nice and new, you could get much more for this room than you're charging me.'

'Yeah, but I'm choosy who I live with. Like I said, I'm happy for you to pay me the same as you pay Olive. Move in whenever you like.'

'Thanks, Jack,' I say. 'You're such a good mate.'

'No problem. Now let's hit the sofa and decide what we're going to get to eat.'

We go back into the lounge and stretch out on a sofa each. Olivia only has one sofa – not that I ever sit in the lounge with her – so sharing with Jack will be easier, as long as he doesn't have a girl here, in which case I'll stay in my room.

'Chinese, Indian or pizza?' Jack asks, scrolling through his phone.

'You choose,' I say. 'I'm happy with any of that.'

'Let's go for Indian, Chicken Balti, yeah?'

'And a Keema Naan.'

'Ordered,' Jack says, tapping and then chucking his mobile onto the coffee table. He jumps up off the sofa and heads to the kitchen, returning moments later with two glasses and a bottle of wine.

'Not for me,' I say. 'I'm not drinking.'

'You've got to have a drink,' Jack says, ignoring me and pouring out two glasses of wine. 'We have to celebrate getting the police out of the way and you moving in here. One glass isn't going to hurt.' He hands me a glass and after a moment's hesitation I take it. I'll just look mealy-mouthed if I refuse it and he's right, one glass isn't going to hurt. I need to learn to drink in moderation like an adult instead of binging like a teenager.

I sip the wine and it tastes so good and I immediately feel the tension ease from my shoulders. I'm looking forward to the food arriving because I haven't eaten much all day and I'm suddenly starving. I sit back and relax for what feels like the first time in ages.

Jack's phone bleeps and he picks it up.

'Food's going to be a bit delayed, should be in here in half-an-hour though, so not too bad for a Friday night.'

Jack refills his wine glass and leans over to top mine up. Somehow the glass is empty and I've drunk it all.

'Not for me, Jack,' I say.

'It's only wine.' He pours me a full glass. 'Two glasses is hardly a binge, is it?'

'I know,' I say, my mouth already watering at the thought of another glass. 'But you know what I'm like once I get the taste for it.'

'You don't have to worry,' Jack says, raising his glass. 'You're with a mate, so it's not as if I'm going to let you get wasted. Cheers!'

I hesitate for a moment before picking up my glass. I study the glass for a moment before slowly raising it in the air.

'Cheers!' I reply.

CHAPTER ELEVEN

I awake and the effort of opening my eyes causes my head to explode. Okay, slight exaggeration, but that's what it feels like. I wonder for the briefest of moments if I have a brain tumour but then reality hits; I have a massive hangover despite the fact that I haven't even been drinking. The room starts to rotate and I remain perfectly still in an attempt to stop it.

Except that I must have been drinking.

I remember having a glass of wine last night and it tasting wonderful and then Jack offering me another. He promised that he wouldn't let me get wasted, so how can this have happened? No way would two glasses of wine give me a hangover like this. I try to remember what happened last night. I recall the curry arriving and I even remember eating it and saying how great it was. I definitely drank the second glass of wine that Jack poured for me, but after that?

Nothing.

Nothing at all, complete blackness.

I concentrate and wait for the flashbacks to start to emerge but they're not forthcoming. Yet. Perhaps they'll come later, they often do but I usually remember *something* when I wake up, even if it's only my drunken dreams.

I don't remember anything after the second glass of wine, I have no idea how I got home or of going to bed. I close my eyes to stop the room from spinning but as soon as I do I feel bile seep into my mouth. I swallow it down, burning my throat. I open my eyes again, which is when I realise.

I'm not in my own bedroom.

I slowly turn my head and the pain isn't as bad as I thought it would be, it's *almost* bearable. I look around to find that I'm in a large room with off-white walls and bland furniture. It doesn't look like a hotel room so I must be in someone's house. There's a large window directly in front of me covered by thick, beige curtains. Weak sunshine is filtering through the curtains, which I guess is what woke me. I wonder what the time is, it could be afternoon for all I know. I slowly turn my head to see my phone lying on the bedside cabinet next to a beige lamp. Wherever I am, they certainly like beige and there's something about the room that's familiar. I contemplate sitting up and seeing what the time is but the effort it will require defeats me.

Where am I?

The duvet feels soft underneath my fingers and I clutch the top of the cover and pull it up in front of my face. Beige, like the rest of the room, but I can feel that it's good quality bedding because it's very soft on my skin.

My skin. All of my skin.

Reality hits and I pull the duvet up and look down to see that I'm naked.

I close my eyes and try not to panic.

I take several deep breathes, force my eyes open and haul myself upright. When the room has stopped spinning I look around; the clothes I was wearing yesterday are neatly folded in a pile on a chair next to a chest of drawers. I must have put them there but I have no recollection of doing so. The feeling of panic threatens to engulf me again; I always have black voids that I can't remember when I've been drinking but I've never forgotten *everything*. Have I had one binge too many and I've permanently damaged my memory? An entire bottle of vodka is enough to kill someone with alcohol poisoning, could I have given myself brain damage? Is that possible? I think it is.

I run my hands down my body as if it will tell me what happened. Did I share this bed with someone?

Did I have sex with someone and I can't even remember?

I feel sick and it's not just because of the hangover; I'm naked in a strange bed and I have no idea where I am or how I got here.

But I'm about to find out.

Because the bedroom door is opening.

I watch from the bed as the familiar figure of Jack comes into the room.

'Hello, you,' he says, with a smile. 'I thought you were never going to wake up.'

I feel a rush of relief that I'm not lying in a random stranger's bed but then the relief vanishes when I realise that I'm in Jack's bed. Why am I in his bed, where did he sleep and why don't I have any clothes on?

'I'm making you breakfast,' he says, sitting down on the end of the bed and rubbing my foot through the duvet. 'But you need to get up. I never eat in bed because I can't stand crumbs on the sheets. It'll be ready in about ten minutes.'

I stare at him and wonder why he isn't moving and why he's rubbing my foot. I don't want any breakfast but more than that, no way am I getting out of bed while he's still in the room. He looks at me for a moment and then leans across and kisses me on the lips. I'm so shocked that I make no move to stop him.

'You've just got time for a quick shower,' he says, as he stands up. 'And you might want to swill some toothpaste around your mouth. Your breath is a bit grim.' He pulls a mock disgusted face and goes back out of the room and thankfully, closes the door.

I stay perfectly still and stare at the closed door.

Oh fuck.

* * *

I'm sitting at Jack's dining table in the clothes that I was wearing last night. I feel slightly less disgusting for having had a hot shower but putting yesterday's underwear on was a new low for me.

But not as low as sleeping with my best mate and remembering absolutely nothing about it.

Jack is bustling around the kitchen, making coffee and getting out plates and knives and forks and behaving as if this is the most natural situation in the world. He's whistling a tuneless song and has a big grin on his face every time he looks over at me.

'You okay, Josie? You're looking a bit serious.' Jack stops what he's doing and looks at me with concern.

'Bit of a headache,' I say.

'Really? Do you want some paracetamol or an ibuprofen?' He doesn't wait for me to answer but goes to a cupboard, rummages around and pulls out a packet. He then opens another cupboard and takes out a glass, fills it with water and brings it over and puts it on the table in front of me. He slides into the chair opposite, takes two tablets from the packet and gives them to me.

'Thanks.'

'If that's what two glasses of wine does, perhaps

you should give it up altogether,' Jack says.

'Was it only two glasses, though?' I ask, as I put the tablets in my mouth and choke them down with nearly a whole glass of water.

'Yeah,' he says, looking a bit puzzled. 'Can't you remember?'

'Of course, I remember,' I lie. 'But they were big glasses, weren't they? Doesn't that count as four?'

'No.' Jack shakes his head. 'They were normal size, there's still some left in the bottle.' He nods at the bottle on the worktop, it's about a third full and it's the bottle he poured the wine from last night.

'You don't regret last night? Do you?' he asks, his eyes searching my face.

I finish the glass to avoid answering but I can't avoid Jack's gaze. He's looking deep into my eyes and he looks so vulnerable and unsure of himself, not the usual Jack at all. I feel like an absolute shit. How can I tell him that I can't even remember?

I can't.

'Of course, I don't.' I say, with a smile.

'Phew,' Jack says, taking hold of my hands. 'That's a relief. You seemed so sure it was what you wanted last night and I couldn't quite believe it. I mean, I've had feelings for you for a long time but I never dreamed that you felt the same way. When you told me how you felt it was like all my Christmases had come at once.'

I try to keep the dismay from my face but inside I'm dying. It's even worse than I thought possible; it's not even a friends-with-benefits sort of thing.

Oh God, what if Jack is in love with me?

'Now.' Jack gets up from the chair. 'A big mug of coffee followed by Jack's special bacon sandwich will set you right and get rid of that headache. Don't move an inch and I'll bring it over.'

I watch as he goes over to the oven, puts on a pair of giant oven gloves, opens the door and pulls out a baking tray with rashers of bacon piled on it. He's not whistling now but humming and he has a smile on his face whilst he butters the bread and makes the sandwiches.

'You like brown sauce?' He turns and holds the bottle up.

'Love it,' I say, wondering if I'll be able to eat it without vomiting.

He brings over two mugs of coffee and returns to the worktop, picks up the plates and brings them to the table. I take a sip of the coffee and then another, the warmth filling my stomach and making me feel marginally better.

Jack takes an enormous bite out of his sandwich and I pick mine up and force myself to nibble it. I chew it and it goes down and hits my stomach but instead of coming straight back up, it settles there. I take another bite and before I know it, I've eaten the first half and am starting on the other. Jack's finished his and is sipping his coffee and looking at me with a smile on his face.

'What?' I ask, mid-bite.

'Just feels a bit weird, doesn't it? What with us having been mates for three years.'

I nod.

'It's good timing really, what with you having to move out of Olive's and everything.' He takes another sip of coffee and I stay quiet because I have no idea what to say.

'That's if you still want to move in,' he says.

'Of course, I do,' I lie. 'Just this headache, you know?' I tap my head to emphasise it and then wish I hadn't.

'Sorry about your headache,' he says, as if it's his fault. 'But it was good, wasn't it? Last night?'

I nod and smile because it's all I can manage.

'And I know this sounds soppy, Josie, but I can say it to you 'cos we know each other so well, but last night was the best night of my life.'

I stare at Jack and try to keep the horror from my face.

'I've been around the block, had quite a few partners,' he says, with a grin. 'But I can honestly say that we get each other, don't we? Sexually, I mean, we clicked, just like that, no messing about. And to think,' he goes on, laughing. 'That I was in such a mood last week because I thought you fancied our new boss. I was so jealous it was eating me up. What a fucking idiot I am.'

OMG it gets worse. He was in a mood because of *me*.

I don't feel the way Jack thinks I do, I don't see him in *that* way and I don't think that I ever will. He's a great friend but I don't fancy him one little bit; not because he's not attractive, because he is, but he's just a mate. I have no idea how last night happened but it was a massive mistake.

I'm lying to myself; I know why last night happened – it was because of alcohol. I might have only had two glasses of wine but last night has confirmed to me that I can never, ever, drink again.

I'm going to have to tell him the truth.

But not today.

I'm going to have to think very carefully about what I'm going to say. I can't tell him the whole truth – that I can't remember anything – because it's beyond insulting. Yet again, my drinking has caused disaster and I have to face the fact that once I tell him I don't feel the same way as he does, our friendship will be ruined.

There'll be no going back after I've told him.

Jack will never speak to me again.

CHAPTER TWELVE

I get back from my trip to the chemist and go straight to my room. Olivia isn't here but I'm making sure that there's no possibility of bumping into her if she suddenly comes back. I close the door and sit on the bed and remove the morning-after pill that I just purchased from my handbag and read the instructions carefully.

I'm not sure whether I actually need to take it but I'm taking no chances. I'm assuming that Jack always practices safe sex but I can hardly ask him, can I? The way my luck's been going lately, I'm making absolutely sure that an unwanted pregnancy isn't thrown into the mix.

Although it's hardly bad luck, is it? It's my own sheer stupidity.

My phone bleeps from the bedside table and I lean over to see a message from Jack pop up.

Hey babe, how u feeling? Do you want me to come over and look after u? xxx

I take the pill out of the packet and stare at it for a moment before swallowing it down dry. It feels as if I'm swallowing a golf ball. I pick my phone up and tap out a reply.

I'm going to bed, I lie, *I'm not great company at the moment and from past experience the best thing I can do is sleep x*

Seconds later he replies.

Okay babe, no worries. Sleep well and see u tomorrow xxx

I don't reply but toss my phone back onto the bedside cabinet where it lands with a clunk. I lie down on the bed and close my eyes.

I'm going to have to tell him.

Yesterday felt like it was never going to end. After we'd eaten breakfast Jack insisted that we go for a walk on the heath because it would help get rid of my headache. What could I say? I felt like a tramp in my day-old work clothes but when I said this he suggested going back to mine and getting changed. No way did I want that because at least at his place I was sort of in control, I could leave whenever I wanted whereas getting him to leave my place would be more difficult.

We tramped around the heath for what felt like hours and then called into the *Dog and Gun* on the way back for a drink. I had orange juice, despite Jack trying to persuade me to have a *hair of the dog that bit me*.

Once we were back at Jack's I went to the toilet and came back and lied that I'd just got my period and needed to go home. There wasn't a lot he could say to that. I then lied some more and told him that it was what was causing my headache and that I suffered quite badly every month.

He seemed very concerned and insisted on calling me a taxi on his account even though I said I was fine to walk. I felt such relief when I got into the taxi that I didn't have to keep up the pretence anymore and then felt immediately shit for thinking like that.

Jack now thinks that I'm bed bound every month because of my periods and I think I've actually made it worse because when I tell him the truth, he's going to know that it was all a lie and that as well as being a near-alcoholic, I'm a big, fat, liar, too.

What a mess.

Maybe I should just be a complete coward and tell him in a message.

But I'd still have to face him at work tomorrow.

I have to think it through carefully before I go making things worse and doing something that can't be undone. So firstly, can I really not be in a relationship with him? He's my best friend so would it really be so terrible because it's not as if he's a totally heartless bastard like Rafe.

I think about it.

Jack's good-looking, he's funny, I can talk to him about anything and we get on really well, despite his moods. On paper, he's pretty much the perfect boyfriend. He has his own flat, a steady job – he's always said that once he meets the right person he'll actually use his degree and get himself a proper career – and he knows everything about me and accepts me, binge-drinking past and crashing weddings included.

So what, Josie, is the problem?

There's no spark of attraction for me at all. It may have ended in disaster but when I was seeing Rafe, I thought about him *all* of the time to the point of obsession. When I wasn't with him, I couldn't wait to see him and when I was with him, I was dreading not being with him.

It's no good; I don't feel that way about Jack.

Maybe we did click in bed, as Jack says, but as I can't remember I'll have to take his word for it. It's no good, he's a mate and to me, that's all he'll ever be.

And that's the last thought in my head as I drift off to sleep.

* * *

The sound of a door closing wakes me.

My room is in semi-darkness and I pick up my phone from the bedside table to see that it's nearly six o'clock. I get up from the bed and go out into the hallway to see that the lounge door is ajar and the lounge light is on.

Good, this means that Olivia is home.

I need to talk and build some bridges with her; there's no way that I can move into Jack's now so I need some time to find another place to live. I'm going to look for a room in a shared house to keep the costs down. I'm also looking to share with more than one person. It'll be an opportunity to meet other people, but more than that, sharing with just one person is too intense and *personal*.

I walk into the lounge and there's no sign of Olivia so I continue into the kitchen. She has her back to me and is standing at the cooker stirring something in a saucepan. I guess she's making herself scrambled eggs because that's all she ever eats apart from when she has her friends over.

'Hi, Olivia, how's it going?' I say, pleasantly.

She jumps slightly at the sound of my voice and I think what a bag of nerves she is. I can't think why I never noticed this when I first viewed the flat; when I look for somewhere new to live I'll be doing it with a lot more experience under my belt. I'll actually be taking notice of what people are like instead of assuming we'll just get along.

'Hi Josephine,' she says, turning to give me a pinched smile before turning back to her stirring.

I bite down my irritation at her using my full name and sit down at the table and clear my throat to let her know that I want to speak to her.

She jumps slightly again and turns to face me.

'I've been thinking,' I say, carefully. 'About me moving out?'

She stares at me and there it is again; the fear.

She's definitely scared of me.

'The thing is,' I say, in a rush to get it over with. 'That I have to find somewhere else so I don't know how long that's going to take. Will that be a big problem?'

She shrugs her shoulders but doesn't answer.

''I mean,' I continue. 'I'll start looking immediately but realistically I have no idea what's available.'

She shrugs again.

'And just so you know, Olivia, I don't know whatever gave you the idea that I'd been in your room, but I can promise you that I haven't and I never would.'

She doesn't shrug this time but stands perfectly rigid.

There's an awkward silence and then Olivia turns to the cooker, flicks off the hob, picks the saucepan up and walks to the countertop and tips the scrambled egg onto the plate. There's nothing else on the plate and I wonder where the toast is. She always has toast. She takes the empty saucepan to the sink and fills it with water and then returns and picks up the plate and the knife and fork next to it and carries it through to the lounge. I give her a minute and then follow her.

I need her to know that I'm not a thief or a snoop. I'm prepared to move out but for some reason, even though I don't like her, I don't want her thinking badly of me. I've done enough bad things without being blamed for stuff I didn't even do.

I stand in the doorway to the lounge and look around in bemusement; she's not in the lounge, which means that she's going to eat in her bedroom.

Probably with the door locked.

I sigh and go back into the lounge and close the door and turn the television on. I've tried but if she doesn't want to sit in here I might as well take advantage of that. The TV in here is much bigger and better than the one in my bedroom. I flick around the channels until I find something non-threatening that requires no effort to watch before going out into the kitchen.

I wash the saucepan up and then crack three eggs into it and add milk. I'm having scrambled eggs too although I'll have toast with mine. I've only had a couple of biscuits since breakfast as I went into town and then came home and fell asleep. I didn't sleep well last night because I was churning everything over in my mind and who knows about the night before?

My stomach churns at the thought of the energetic sex I might have had with Jack. Who knows what I did, because I certainly don't. I put it out of my mind and focus on stirring the eggs and putting bread in the toaster.

I take my plate into the lounge when the eggs and toast are ready and sit on the sofa and eat it while watching a period drama that I have absolutely no interest in. I then go back out into the kitchen and wash and dry the dishes and put them away and wipe the worktops over as if I'm auditioning to be the perfect housemate.

I spend the rest of the evening staring at the TV but not really watching it and when it gets to half-past-nine I think about going to bed. If I can manage to get to sleep, maybe I can stop thinking about everything.

I pick up my phone and stare at it; Jack hasn't texted me since this afternoon so he probably thinks that I'm asleep. I feel sad when I think about our friendship being over but a part of me thinks that maybe it's the shove I need; I need to make more friends and not rely on him all the time.

I have to tell him and I'm going to take the cowards way out and message him. I open up WhatsApp and begin to type. I type and delete, type and delete, until I finally end up with:

Hi Jack. There's no easy way to say this so I'm just going to come right out with it. I'm sorry, but although I love you as a friend, that's all you'll ever be to me. I don't feel the same way you do about me. I'm so sorry that I gave you the wrong impression but we've been mates for a long time and I can't lie to you. You're a great guy and I hope that we can still be mates but I wouldn't blame you if you don't ever want to speak to me again. Josie x

It still doesn't sound right, but it's never going to, is it?

I stare at the message for a moment and then before I can stop myself, I press *send.*

It's done.

CHAPTER THIRTEEN

I think I woke up every hour last night, maybe more, and each time I woke, I checked my phone.

Nothing.

The message I sent to Jack was marked as *read* seconds after I sent it, so I know that Jack has seen it, so why hasn't he replied? I was sure that he'd reply, even it was just to have a go at me or tell me to *fuck off,* because I totally deserve it. Jack isn't the type of person who takes things lying down, he always has plenty to say for himself and he's not afraid to come right out and say exactly what he thinks.

So I must have really hurt him.

I couldn't feel any worse if I tried, and now, as well as feeling like a complete shit, I'm also worried about him.

What if he's done something stupid?

Of course, he hasn't, the sensible part of me says, you're not that fabulous that he's going to top himself because you don't want to be his girlfriend. Despite knowing this, I check his WhatsApp status and am relieved to see that he was last active ten minutes ago.

Get over yourself, Josephine Burrows, you're not the love of his, or anyone else's, life.

Now I have to face him at work and the thought is almost enough to make me call in sick but I can't stay off work forever, I'll have to face him sooner or later.

I get up and get showered and dressed and even make myself some sandwiches. Maybe I should look for another job as well as somewhere else to live. My job isn't *that* great; when I started there three years ago I intended using it as a stepping stone to a better job within the company because there are always lots of opportunities on the internal job boards. Laziness, Rafe, and my binge-drinking got in the way so I've never bothered but there's nothing to stop me now.

Maybe all that's happened is the push that I needed; maybe I can turn all these negatives into a positive, as the lifestyle gurus always spout.

I pack my lunchbox into my bag and put my coat on and grab the umbrella from the hallway on the way out. It's raining outside but I'm still going to walk to work rather than wait for a bus that's going to be so packed that I won't get a seat. There's no sign of Olivia this morning so I least I don't have to stomach her frightened rabbit impression. I leave the flat and walk down the stairs and out into the blustery rain. I've hardly got to the end of the street before I dispense with the umbrella as the wind is intent on blowing it inside out. It's not raining too much and I pull the hood up on my Barbour coat to save my hair from the worst of it. I wouldn't normally wear this coat to work because it was expensive and I kept it for casual wear but really, what was I saving it for? I always used to wear my blue coat but who knows where that ended up after I wore it to Rafe's wedding.

All too soon I arrive at work. A small part of me hopes that Jack will take the day off but the braver part of me just wants to get it over with, although I don't know how it's going to work with him sitting opposite me. If it's too awkward, I could ask Damien if I can move to another desk. There's no business reason for Jack and I to sit close together, other people in the office have moved desks and it's not been a problem.

I call out *good morning* as I walk through the office and I can see straightaway that Jack's not in but I wasn't expecting him to be because he's never in before nine. I take my coat off and settle down at my desk as if this is just a normal day but every time the door opens, I jump and my heart starts to pound.

Just when I think that he's not coming in, he breezes into the office with minutes to spare and like a coward, I look down at my keyboard as he makes his way up the office. When I hear him sit down at his desk I look up with a fixed smile on my face and prepare for the worst. I'm expecting to see him with a face like thunder but am shocked to see him grinning at me.

'Morning,' he says, turning his PC on. 'Bloody vile out, isn't it?'

'It is,' I agree. Is this how we're going to play it – pretend that Friday night never happened to save embarrassment all round? Maybe it is. I can do that, much easier than talking about it.

And so begins the longest and strangest day.

Jack behaves as if Friday night never happened, he makes no mention of it at all and nor do I. He's absolutely his old, normal self and I try to be the same. But it's a strain. As the day goes on I want to shout at him to just bloody say something and stop behaving as if everything is okay.

It seems that I can't, as I thought, just pretend that Friday night never happened.

I can't say anything to him about it in the office because there are thirty-six people listening who would just love a bit of fresh, juicy gossip to chew over and digest. By the time the clock has inched its excruciating way to five o'clock, I've decided that I'm going to make sure we leave the office together so I can speak to him about it and get it out in the open. Carrying on as if nothing has happened is just too weird.

'You walking, Jack?' I ask, as we log off and close

our screens down for the day.

'Yeah,' he says, pulling his jacket on. 'As long as it's not pissing down.'

I glance out of the large windows that run the length of the office.

'No, it's stopped. For now.'

'Nice coat,' he says, as we hurry down the stairs.

I smile and wonder if he remembers what happened to my other one. We emerge onto the street and I know that I have to be quick, because it's only a short distance and then we go in different directions.

'Jack,' I start to say.

'Hang on, Josie, stop for a minute.' He puts his hand in his jacket pocket and fumbles around. 'I've got something for you.'

I stop and stare and wonder what it is. The bizarre thought that he's bought me a ring flashes across my mind and I tell myself again, to get over myself.

'Here it is.' He holds up a *Star Wars* key ring with one key dangling from it. 'Your door key.'

I stare at it, acknowledging that it is a ring of sorts.

'Jack,' I say. 'I feel really bad about what's happened and I don't expect to move into yours, not now.'

'Why not?' He looks surprised. 'I still need someone to help with the rent.'

'Yeah,' I say, 'But, it's a bit awkward now, what with Friday...' he waves his hand to stop me talking.

'Yeah, about that. Look, I got a bit carried away with it all, I mean, don't get me wrong, Friday night was great, I mean the sex was really great but truthfully, I'm not ready to settle down just yet.'

'You're not?' I look up at him.

'No, I'm not, and quite honestly.' He bites his bottom lip and looks embarrassed. 'I'm glad you sent that text 'cos I think I went a bit over the top. I mean, I can cope with *friends with benefits* but that's about all I'm capable of.'

I stare at him and study his expression to see if he's just trying to save face but if he is, he'd hardly want me moving into his flat.

'Sorry.' He grins. 'If I gave you the wrong idea. Anything more than that is beyond me.'

He's almost making it sound as if *I'm* the one who was wanting a relationship and he's letting me down. Although this is a massive relief, I can't help feeling a bit annoyed. I don't *do* friends with benefits, sex has to mean something for me. At the very least I have to remember it.

'There'll be no *friends with benefits* from me,' I say, with an answering grin, just so there are no misunderstandings.

'Understood.' He points his fingers at his forehead in the scout salute. 'Completely.'

He jiggles the key and I take it from him.

'Just so you know, I'm taking it off the *Star Wars* key ring because that's just tragic,' I say, as I tuck it into my handbag.

'Whatever,' he says, with a grin. 'No doubt you'll put some girly shit on it.'

'Oh, I will, mate,' I say. 'That's a given.'

* * *

Olivia isn't in and I relax in the lounge and reflect on the day's events. However I was expecting Jack to behave, it wasn't anything like that. I'm obviously not as irresistible as I thought I was and Jack is adept at flattering a girl to make her feel like she really matters. Whilst I was imagining he was professing his undying love for me, I'd forgotten that he has a different girl staying over every weekend. Now I feel embarrassed about the text I sent him because I must have misinterpreted what he was saying because he seems fine about it.

I think the best thing to do is to forget all about Friday night and carry on as if it never happened.

Which is easy to do because I can't remember any of it.

I make myself some pasta with a tomato sauce out of a jar and as I wait for it to cook, I decide that I *am* going to start applying for different jobs within the company. I had a search on the internal website at lunchtime and there are several positions that I'm more than qualified for that are several bands above my current pay grade. I need to get a career and do something with my life.

I dish the pasta into a bowl and chuck the saucepan in the sink and fill it with water. I pick up the pasta and a fork and take it into the lounge to eat it and have just sat down when the doorbell rings.

I look at my watch; six-forty-five.

I'm not expecting anyone; I'm never expecting anyone because I have a sad, lonely life and I need to change that, too. I put the pasta on the coffee table, go out into the hallway and pad along to the front door. I silently lean towards the door and put my eye to the spy hole and look out into the corridor.

A man and a woman are standing side by side and I guess that they're Jehovah's Witnesses by their smart suits and the man's neatly cut hair. No way am I going to answer the door.

I pad as quietly as I can back to the lounge and have just sat down when the bell rings again. I pick up my bowl of pasta from the coffee table and am about to tuck in when the bell rings again. This time it rings for a bit longer and I realise that they're not going to go away. I put my bowl down again with a sigh and go back out into the hallway and by the time I reach the front door, the bell has been rung again and I feel my irritation rise. I put the safety chain across and unlock the door and open it several inches.

'Yes?' I say, with a scowl.

'Josephine Burrows?' The woman asks with the hint of a smile.

They can't be Jehovah's Witnesses if she knows my name. I give her a questioning look and she holds a card through the gap in the door.

'DS Hammond and my colleague here is DC Sullivan. I wonder if we might come in?'

I stare through the gap at them and the horrific thought pops into my head that something has happened to Mum and Dad because they always come in pairs to deliver bad news. I should have visited them more often because now it's too late and I'll never see them again.

'Please, it's nothing to worry about,' she says, seeing the horror on my face. 'We just have a few questions we need to ask you.'

'Questions?' My mouth is suddenly dry. 'About what?'

'If you could let us in?' she repeats. 'And then we can discuss it.'

I close the door and unhook the chain and then open it again.

'But I've already answered all the questions at work, I don't know anything else.'

She looks at me with a puzzled expression and turns to her colleague and a look passes between them.

'I'm sorry, I don't know anything about that, Ms Burrows. We're here making enquiries about Mr and Mrs Rafe Bingham and the threats that you've made to them.'

CHAPTER FOURTEEN

My pasta is congealing in the bowl and as I sit on the chair opposite the two police officers on the sofa, I can't understand why Rafe has waited two weeks to report me. I know he's been on his honeymoon but why bother now? And I didn't make any threats to them so how can he have reported me?

Or did I threaten them and I've forgotten? Because I spent a night having sex with my best friend and I can't remember a thing about that.

'Ms Burrows, is it correct that you went to Springton church on Saturday September 29th and interrupted Mr and Mrs Bingham's wedding?' DC Sullivan asks. He doesn't smile and he studies me as if I'm something to be examined, which I suppose I am.

'Aren't you supposed to read me my rights?' I

ask.

There's a hint of a smile from him now.

'We're not arresting you, Ms Burrows, we're simply asking you some questions about certain events.'

'So I don't have to answer if I don't want to?' I ask.

'No, you're under no obligation to answer our questions.'

'In that case.' I stand up. 'I'd like you to leave now.'

'We can leave,' DC Hammond says, with a glance at her colleague. 'But it would be better for you if you answered our questions on an informal basis, rather than us having to take you in to the station.'

'Take me in?' I stare at them in surprise. 'I didn't think crashing a wedding was an offence. Maybe I shouldn't have done it but it's hardly the crime of the century, I didn't actually hurt anyone.'

I hope.

'It's not an offence as such,' DC Hammond says. 'Although it could be construed as disturbing the peace.'

'Or being drunk and disorderly,' DC Sullivan adds.' As you were extremely inebriated.'

I bite my tongue and say nothing.

'Mr and Mrs Bingham were fully prepared to let that matter go. They had no intention of getting the police involved but as events have unfolded they've had to revise their opinion.'

'I have no idea what you're talking about.'

'Okay, Ms Burrows, we'll cut to the chase,' DC Sullivan says, impatiently. 'Mr and Mrs Bingham returned from their honeymoon to find that they'd received a lot of post while they'd been away. Ten threatening letters and three envelopes containing dog excrement, to be precise. Not a very nice thing to come home to, it is?'

I gawp at them both.

'That's absolutely nothing to do with me.'

'The threatening letters tell a different story.' He puts his hand into his coat pocket and pulls out a notebook, opens it and begins to read. 'You both deserve to die. He's a cheat and a liar, don't trust him. He cheated on me, he'll cheat on you.'

I stare at him in disbelief. 'But I never sent them, why would I?'

'Er, the same reason you crashed the wedding?' he asks, with a sneer.

'But it wasn't me,' I insist. 'I've never sent anyone a threatening letter in my life.'

'I could go on and tell you the contents of all of the letters,' he says, ignoring me. 'But they're all in the same vein and obviously you know what's in them because you sent them.'

'You can't say that,' I say. 'That's slander.' Or something like that, I'm not sure what exactly but surely they can't say that I've done something without any evidence.

DC Sullivan has the hint of a smile on his face again and I decide that I'd quite like to remove it by punching him.

'The thing is, Ms Burrows, they *sound* like you wrote them because they contain certain details about your relationship with Mr Bingham. They've all been posted from this area, too.'

'Anyone could have posted them,' I say. 'You don't have any proof at all. A handwriting expert will prove without a doubt that I didn't write those letters.'

'They were printed, Ms Burrows,' DC Hammond says. 'And we were hoping that we wouldn't need to obtain proof.'

'What?' I demand. 'You think I'm just going to own up to something I didn't do?'

'Ms Burrows,' DC Hammond says quietly. 'Mr and Mrs Bingham, and the police, were hoping that an informal warning would be sufficient for you to stop sending the letters and prevent further action needing to be taken.'

'But I didn't do it,' I say, loudly.

They stare at me without speaking and I feel sudden rage at the unfairness of it all. It's bad enough being called a thief by your snowflake flatmate without being accused of sending poison pen letters.

Who would do this to me?

A sudden thought strikes me and the more I think about it, the more sure I become.

'Maybe Mr Bingham sent them to himself to get me into trouble,' I state, firmly. I'm met with blank stares.

'It would be easy enough to do, wouldn't it?' I

ask.

'And why,' DC Hammond asks. 'Would Mr Bingham do that?'

'Because he's a bastard,' I say. 'And it's just the sort of sneaky thing he would do to get his revenge on me for crashing his stupid wedding. He'd think there was some sort of poetic justice to it.' He would, too, and he'd also love bragging to his Hooray Henry mates about how clever he was getting his own back on me for marring his wedding day. I lived with him for over a year, I know *exactly* what he's like. This is a man who sent take-away deliveries and cabs to an acquaintance's house for weeks on end because he'd had the audacity to make a snide comment about him on Facebook. Sending threatening letters and dog shit and blaming me is just his style.

God, what did I ever see in him?

'And how would he be able to post these letters whilst he was in the Maldives, Ms Burrows?' DC Sullivan asks, with the hint of a sneer.

I open my mouth and then close it again. It's pointless, there's no way they're going to believe me. All I can do is hope that now Rafe has had his fun, he's going to stop. If he doesn't, I'm going to end up in court for a crime that I didn't commit.

'I think we'll leave it there, Ms Burrows,' DC Sullivan says, standing up. 'And let's hope that we don't have any reason to visit you again.'

I stand up and pull myself up as tall as someone of five-foot-five can, but I still feel like a naughty schoolchild. DC Sullivan heads towards the door and DC Hammond gets up and follows him, giving me a slightly sympathetic smile as she goes. I follow them out into the hallway and open the front door.

'Oh, one last thing,' DC Sullivan says, mid-stride through the doorway. 'Why did you think we were here about a work-related matter?'

'Oh nothing,' I say, sounding pathetically unconvincing. 'I just got a bit confused.'

He frowns and scrutinises my face and I just know that he's going to go straight back to the station and check my name, so I'll look even more of a liar.

I watch as they walk down the corridor to make sure they've gone and then close the door firmly behind them and go back into the lounge. My dish of congealed pasta stares at me from the coffee table and I walk over to it, pick it up, and hurl it at the wall with all of my strength.

* * *

'I can't do anything, can I? I'm stuck, because I already look like a psycho for crashing the wedding. All I can hope is that Rafe stops doing it and blaming me.'

Jack rubs his chin, inhales deeply from his cigarette then blows a stream of smoke up into the air. He's standing on the balcony smoking and I'm sitting on the sofa as far away as I can get from the open doors. He said he needs to smoke to think of a plan but I've told him there's nothing we can do; if I go anywhere near Rafe I'll be arrested. I just wish he'd hurry up and finish and come in, just the sight of all six-foot-four of him standing by the glass balcony surround is enough to set my nerves on edge. He's so tall the top railing only reaches the tops of his legs and I keep having a vision of him stumbling and then toppling over the rail to his death.

He takes a last drag and then stubs his cigarette out in the fire bucket on the floor of the balcony, comes inside and closes and locks the door.

'You might as well smoke it in here,' I grumble. 'The whole place stinks now.'

'Bloody hell, you've got a right mare on, haven't you?' Jack throws himself onto the other sofa.

'Sorry,' I say. 'I'm a miserable cow. I'm just so pissed off about that prick. He couldn't let me have the last word, could he? It's not enough to dump me and then marry someone else after he's been with her for five minutes, he has to get the police after me as well.'

I pull my legs up onto the sofa and wrap my arms around them, and rest my head on my knees. I look across at Jack and he's deep in thought again and I want to tell him not to bother, because there's absolutely nothing I can do. I can't contact Rafe in any way at all or else he'll accuse me of stalking him, I'm well and truly stuck. I don't bother saying this to Jack because he'll figure it out for himself.

I'm just so grateful that we're still friends and I was able to come round here and unload it all. I think I'd have gone mad if I hadn't been able to talk to someone.

My temper got the better of me when I hurled the pasta and now there's a red stain on the lounge wall because, despite all my scrubbing and using every cleaner that I could lay my hands on underneath the sink, it won't come off. When Olivia sees it she's probably going to think that I murdered someone and it's their blood. And she'll notice there's a bowl missing too, even though I've buried it at the bottom of the bin.

'What if you talked to him?' Jack says. 'Apologised for crashing his wedding?'

'What?' I shout. 'You must be joking. I'd rather go to prison for ten years than apologise to that prick.'

'I'm joking,' Jack says, with a grin. 'You're so easy to wind up. You know I hate his guts, too. I take it you're completely over him now?'

'I am, can't think what I ever saw in him, the arrogant, posh, entitled prick.'

'But seriously, Josie, I don't think you need to worry. He's going to stop because if he doesn't, you'll end up in court, right?'

'Yeah,' I say, slowly, not understanding what he's getting at.

'Well, if you get charged and you end up in court, *he'll* have to go to court to testify against you, won't he?'

Jack's right, he will, and Rafe won't want to appear in court or have his face splashed over the local newspaper. Revenge is one thing, publicity is another. He won't want his reputation associated in any way, shape or form with a mad, ex-girlfriend stalker, even if he is the victim. It won't be good for the family's fancy advertising agency if every time Rafe's name is Googled, a stalker case came up.

'You could be right,' I say.

'I'm always right,' Jack says, picking up the TV remote control.

'Not always,' I say.

'Tell me when I've ever been wrong.'

I think about it and annoyingly, I can't think of anything. I'm sure there must have been a time when he was wrong but I can't remember when. I feel a bit better now because I think he is right, Rafe's had his fun and I've been suitably humiliated so fingers crossed, it's all over.

Jack flicks around the channels and lands on the local evening news, which is when I realise the time.

'I didn't realise it was so late,' I say. 'I'd better call a cab because I'm not walking home in the dark.'

'Stay the night,' Jack says, casually. 'Your room's all ready, you could start moving your stuff in next weekend, if you like.'

I think about it for a moment; again, annoyingly, he's right. The sooner I move the better, because Olivia's going to be even worse once she spots the tomato sauce on the wall.

'I won't stay the night,' I say. 'Because I haven't got a change of clothes with me. I can't turn up for work looking like a tramp but I think you're right about moving in next weekend.'

Jack flaps his hand and I realise his eyes are fixed on the TV and the hand flap is to tell me to be quiet. I can see I'm going to have to fight for the TV remote when I move in. I turn to the TV just in time to see a picture of Evelyn vanish from the screen.

'...police have today confirmed that the local man helping them with their enquiries into the murder of Evelyn Pemberton has been released without charge. A spokesperson has confirmed that they have received information that Ms Pemberton was believed to have been in an altercation with a woman on the evening of her murder. The police are asking members of the public to think back to the night of the 29th September and if they were in the vicinity of Tudor Walk. They may have seen something that didn't mean anything at the time but could be related to the incident. If you have any further information please contact your local police station as soon as possible. In other news...'

Every bit of saliva dries in my mouth and I face the truth.

It's all unravelling because someone, somewhere, will have seen me shouting at Evelyn.

I'm done for.

CHAPTER FIFTEEN

There's a saying that no news is good news.

Since the police announcement that they were investigating a report of Evelyn having an altercation with an unknown woman on the evening of her death, I've heard nothing. But it didn't feel like a good thing to me; it was five days of waiting for the knock on the door and jumping at every noise and not sleeping for worrying and thinking about it. It got to the point where I was seriously thinking about calling the police and giving myself up just to get it over with. It was Jack who stopped me. What, he said, were the chances of the police knowing it was me with no CCTV, the vaguest of descriptions that could apply to half the population and the fact that it happened over three weeks ago? Zero, he said, adding that the police were obviously grasping at straws because they had no leads or evidence at all. I gave some serious thought to what he said and decided that my life would be much easier if I chose to believe him and take his advice and amazingly, once I made that decision, I started to feel better.

Besides wasting time worrying, this week has been super busy. I've come home from work every night and gradually packed up all of my belongings so that I'm ready to move into Jack's flat today. I don't have any furniture to move so it's purely personal possessions, but it's amazing how much stuff I've accumulated over the years. Whilst I've been packing it all, I've made a concerted effort to get rid of stuff that I don't need. I've been quite ruthless and any clothes that I haven't worn for a year have been taken to the charity shop and donated. The top drawer of my chest of drawers used to be filled with makeup but it'll now fit into one small zip-up cosmetic bag, because there really is no point in keeping dried up mascaras and worn-down lipsticks.

It's felt quite cathartic too, because most of the clothes that I wore when Rafe and I were together are now gone. I never wore them anymore because I didn't want to be reminded of him. Arguably, it could be seen as a bit of a waste as they were expensive designer stuff but I couldn't bear the thought of actually wearing them. I debated selling them on eBay and putting the proceeds towards my deposit savings, but then thought that giving them to charity was the better thing to do. It's a sort of a penance for all the bad stuff that I've done lately and makes me feel slightly better about myself. It was wasteful buying designer clothes just to impress a man when I should have been saving that money for a deposit on a house but that's a lesson learned; never again.

Even though I've got rid of a lot of stuff, what I have left will still fill an average car. I intended hiring a car to take it all to Jack's place because I know a cab driver won't be impressed with me filling his cab up with it all. I moved it all to Olivia's in a cab and the driver was so unpleasant and snotty about it even though I gave him a massive tip. It's not as if he even helped me carry it or anything, he just looked on while I shoved it all in and then got it all out again while pointedly looking at his watch the whole time.

I've never owned a car, or even wanted to, because I can walk or get a bus easily around here but I took lessons and passed my test when I was eighteen. I thought it would be useful for the day when I decided to buy a car.

Probably one of the few sensible things that I've done in my life.

I was a bit nervous about driving a hire car. I drove Rafe's car a few times when he was too pissed to drive and I've driven my brother, Nick's car, now and then, but I'm hardly what you call an experienced driver. When I told Jack my plan he looked at me as if I was mad. Why was I hiring a car, he asked, when he had one? I was gobsmacked when he said it; I never knew he had a car and I've known him for three years. I've never known him to drive anywhere and he always gets the bus or walks to work. How could he have a car without me knowing about it? He laughed and said he rarely uses it but keeps it parked in the underground car park of the flats. He only uses it when he visits his parents in London or needs to drive out of town.

Something else I never knew about; the underground car park, I'd never even noticed it. Jack says I must go through life with my eyes closed because *there's a bloody great ramp going down to it and you walk past it every time you come over*. I think he's right, I need to wake up a bit and take more notice of everything and stop drifting along in a daydream.

So, all of my worldly belongings are packed into two suitcases, three boxes and too many *bags for life* to count. It's all sitting ready in the hallway and I'm just waiting for Jack to arrive. Olivia has already gone out for the day even though it's only half-past-nine. I finished packing everything last night so that I wouldn't have to get up at the crack of dawn and when I got up at eight this morning, Olivia was nowhere to be seen. She'd left a note on the kitchen worktop asking me to leave the key when I left and that was it; no good wishes, no niceties or anything even remotely friendly. I can't help feeling pissed off; she might be having some sort of breakdown but she could at least be pleasant about me leaving. It's not my fault she's imagining things.

My mobile bleeps and I open it to see a message from Jack.

I'm here. Be up in a minute.

He makes no mention of the fact that's he's half-an-hour later than he said he'd be, although I'm hardly going to say anything as he's doing me a big favour. I go out to the hall, open the front door and drag all of my stuff outside and then go back into the kitchen and place my front door key next to her note.

Goodbye Olivia

* * *

'Christ,' Jack says, as he starts the engine. 'I thought you said you'd had a good sort out. I've never seen so much crap in my life.'

I glance over my shoulder at the back seat of the car which is filled with a jumble of *bags for life* and cardboard boxes. I also have a bag wedged by my feet. The suitcases are in the boot with barely an inch to spare and Jack had to practically sit on the lid to get it closed. From the minute Jack arrived I've felt a tension in the air and I'm not quite sure why. Maybe he's ratty because he's late. The thought crosses my mind that he had a girl staying over last night and I've dragged him out of bed and ruined his sex life.

'You never told me you had a tiny car,' I say, trying not to sound petulant. 'I would have hired one if I'd known it was so small.'

'It's not small,' he says. 'It's a normal-sized car. Perfectly adequate for a normal person's possessions.'

'So I'm not normal now?' I ask, in an offended tone.

Jack laughs and I feel the tension in the air ease ever so slightly. 'About as normal as I am,' he says.

We pull up to the traffic lights and I look around the car and then lean forward and flick the radio on. Only it's not the radio, it's a CD player and I listen in surprise as Mariah Carey starts to belt out *all I want for Christmas is you.*

'Never took you for a Mariah Carey fan,' I say, with a snort.

Jack frowns and reaches across and turns the CD player off.

'I never use that, I've got my own music on my mobile. It must be my mum's.'

'Oh,' I say.

'This used to be my mum's car. She gave it to me when she got a new one.'

'Oh, I see.' Now it all makes sense; when Jack said he had a car I never imagined him driving a *Renault Clio* because he's six-foot-four and has legs that go on forever. No wonder he doesn't drive it very much because even with the driver's seat pushed so far back that it's rammed into the rear passenger seat, his knees are still practically touching his chest. That fact that it was his mum's also explains the pink air freshener with a picture of a cat on it hanging from the mirror. It must be a good one because I can still smell the strawberry scent coming from it.

'I hardly use it so it's not worth trading it in for something bigger,' he says. 'It's cheap to run and costs me next to nothing so I can't complain.'

'It's brilliant,' I say. 'A really nice car.'

After a few seconds of silence we burst into laughter at my insincere comment and we zoom off as the lights turn green.

* * *

Somehow, we managed to get all of my stuff into the lift in one go. Once we reached the sixth floor, we ferried it all along the corridor and into my new bedroom in Jack's flat. Although to be fair, Jack did the majority of the donkey work while I carried the *bags for life*.

Once everything is dumped in my room, Jack disappears and goes back downstairs to park the car. I start unpacking and as I open the cases on the bed I realise how little storage space there is in this room. The wardrobe is half the size of the one that I had at Olivia's and there's only one chest of drawers whereas I used to have two. There's plenty of space in the room to fit in more furniture, so I could buy another wardrobe. It wouldn't be a waste of money because I can take it with me when

I buy my own house.

I fill the chest of drawers and wardrobe in no time at all and then hang the remaining clothes from the top of each end of the wardrobe. I still have shoes that I can't fit in anywhere so I stack them inside one of the empty cardboard boxes and put it next to the chest of drawers. I can always buy some sort of shoe rack or maybe even one of those plastic storage boxes once I'm settled.

I carry one of the bags into the ensuite and look around in delight; I can leave whatever I like in here with no one else using it or moving it around or just plain nosing through my stuff. I fill the shelves with my lotions and potions and hang my fluffy, yellow towels on the rack. There's already a white bath and hand towel on there so I take them off and fold them carefully to give back to Jack.

There. Much more homely and cosy.

I feel quite pleased with myself as all I have left to unpack is my stuff to go in the kitchen. I pick up the last two bags and carry them through to the kitchen. Jack still isn't back and I wonder what can be taking him so long because he's been gone for ages. I check my watch to see that it's nearly twelve o'clock – which means he's been gone for an hour-and-a-half. I start opening cupboard doors, wondering which cupboards are for me. Each cupboard is super tidy with everything neatly aligned, even the cans of food are neatly arranged so that all of the labels point the same way. I had two cupboards to myself at Olivia's and the middle shelf of the fridge, although it was a bit of a squeeze fitting everything in.

'What are you looking for?'

I jump at the sound of Jack's voice. I didn't hear him come in.

'Christ,' I say. 'You'll give me a heart attack. Where have you been?'

'Putting the car away,' he says, flatly. 'What are you looking in all the cupboards for?'

'An empty cupboard?' I say. 'To put my stuff in?'

He walks over to the one door that I haven't tried and pulls it open.

'Great,' I say, even though it's nowhere near enough room for me. I start taking tins from my bag and sliding them onto the shelves. 'Which one can I use for my other bits? And what shelf shall I use in the fridge?'

'What other stuff?' There's that frown again.

'Mugs, plates, bits and bobs,' I say. My sandwich toaster, my special omelette pan, my extra big wine glasses that I'm never going to use, to name but a few items.

'You won't need any of that,' Jack says. 'I've got everything you need. I haven't really got room for random crap.'

There's that word again, *crap*. My stuff isn't crap, I've thrown all the *crap* away and I don't like Jack implying that my stuff is some sort of rubbish.

'You can have the middle shelf of the fridge and I thought we could just share the racking in the door,' Jack says, pulling open the fridge.

'Okay,' I say. I have nothing to actually put in there as I need to go shopping. I deliberately haven't bought anything this week so I wouldn't have to bring it with me. I've left Olivia the gift of half a bottle of milk and one egg.

I decide that another cupboard for my *random crap* is a discussion for another day and I resume putting my canned food in the cupboard as Jack stands and watches me. I drag the bagful of bits and pieces – or crap as Jack calls it – over to the corner of the kitchen and shove it underneath the table.

'What are you doing?'

'Putting it out of the way.'

'You can't leave it there,' Jack says. 'It looks a right mess.'

I stay silent but pull the bag back out, pick it up and carry it through to my bedroom. Jack follows me and watches from the doorway as I park the bag next to my bag of shoes. I see his gaze travel around the room and settle on the wardrobe.

'Why haven't you put your clothes in the wardrobe?' he asks.

'I have.'

'So why have you got everything hanging on the outside?'

'Because,' I say, as I walk towards him. 'The wardrobe isn't big enough to fit everything inside.'

'But it looks a right mess.' He frowns. Again. 'Proper untidy. I can't stand mess.'

'Well, that's fine,' I say, grasping hold of the door

handle. 'Because this is my room now and you won't have to look at it.'

He stares at me for a moment and I stare right back.

'Now if you don't mind, Jack, I've got stuff to do.' And I close the door gently, but firmly, in his face.

For God's sake.

He's worse than my mother.

CHAPTER SIXTEEN

Damien is leaving us.

He came out of his office on Monday morning and announced that another temporary replacement for Evelyn has been found and he's returning to his role as Financial Controller. It was a bit of a surprise as he's only been here a matter of weeks and we'd all got used to him and thought he might be staying for a while. Everyone's a bit fed up about it – except for Jack, who's delighted and says that Damien is an arse – especially as Damien's not hanging around and his last day will be on Friday. He's asked us all to join him for a drink after work, though, and even Jack's going because he says there's no way he'll pass on a free drink. I'll go but it'll be strictly orange juice for me; the memory, or should I say non-memory, of my night in Jack's bed is enough to remind me that I can never touch alcohol again. I still can't remember a single thing about it, although I'm not sure if that's good or bad.

By Tuesday afternoon – yesterday – Darla had found out through a mate in HR that the reason Damien was leaving us so soon was because his deputy was making a right hash of running *his* department. They needed him back, pronto, because the year-end figures need to be presented to the board and they need to be right. Wrong figures mean wrong bonuses and the big bosses definitely wouldn't want that. The word is that Damien's replacement is a dinosaur from the company statistics department who's worked here forever and needs to be moved on to make way for fresh blood. No doubt our new manager will be *temporary* until the day he draws his retirement pension.

I do feel a bit sad that Damien's leaving because he's seems like a genuinely nice guy and I get on really well with him; everyone does, actually, except for Jack who can barely look at him without sneering. Jack's remark that he felt jealous of Damien talking to me keeps popping into my head even though I don't want it to and has made me feel a bit self-conscious about talking to him in front of Jack. I have to remind myself that Jack has the gift of the gab and probably says something similar to all of the girls that he talks into bed and that it's just talk. The more I think about it, the more I realise that Jack *must* have sweet talked me into bed because despite being wasted, I have no feelings towards him at all except as a mate.

Jack.

Hmm. Let's just say that before I moved in with him, I had no idea what a neat freak he was. I always thought his place was tidy when I went round but I never realised how over the top he is; I mean *really* over the top. I've had to massively up my game to make sure that I wipe up every single crumb when I make myself some toast, and the plate and knife have to go in the dishwasher the very *minute* that I've finished with them and not be left lying around on the worktop. He couldn't find the remote control one evening because I'd left it on the sofa and it got tucked between the cushions and I honestly thought he was going to cry.

I'm making sure to keep my bedroom door closed at all times because I don't think Jack will be able to cope if he can see inside. It's not that I'm massively untidy but I leave the duvet pulled back at the end of the bed all day and I'm not averse to leaving a few clothes lying around. Not on the floor though, because I'm not a slob. I'm finding his fastidiousness slightly annoying but I remind myself that it could be much worse, at least he's not accusing me of snooping in his room or stealing from him. And although I don't like it, I'd rather he did his frowning thing than look at me like a terrified rabbit the way Olivia did. And being super neat isn't such a bad thing, is it? If I was living with a disgusting slob I'd really have something to moan about. Rafe never lifted a finger to do anything; as soon as I moved in with him he seemed to think that I would do all of the cooking, washing and cleaning. Stupidly, I did, in my desperation to make him love me.

Aside from the over-tidiness, Jack and I are getting along fine and despite the forgotten night in his bed I haven't felt uncomfortable with him at all, we have the same easy friendship that we've always had. It's nice to watch TV with someone in the evening instead of spending most of the time on my own in my room. I'm still going to save hard for a deposit and get my own place, though, because I think it's about time I grew up and did something.

I've heard nothing more from the police about Rafe and the poison pen letters so, fingers crossed, Rafe's had his fun and is going to leave me alone. I do feel enraged when I think about him and the way he's got one over on me but I'll just have to suck it up because if I go near him, I'll be arrested and charged.

I've also been checking online every day and there's been nothing new reported about Evelyn's murder – although they have appealed again for the woman she was seen talking with to come forward. That's how it was worded, *talking with*, not *in an altercation with* like they said on TV last week. I'm wondering if it's going to be one of those murders that never gets solved, because it's been weeks now and they still haven't arrested anyone. What if I was the last person to see her alive? I looked on Google maps and Tudor Walk is only a couple of streets away from her house and the next street back from the church. I didn't realise her house was so close to the church but then why would I? Did I meet her there by chance after I left the church? I wish I could remember; if I could remember then I could go to the police and tell them about it and then I wouldn't have to worry about it anymore but because of the stupid black hole in my memory, I can't.

I'm never, ever, drinking again.

I might even be able to help catch the murderer if I could remember anything about it. Maybe someone was watching or hanging around and I saw them; maybe it was sheer luck that Evelyn was murdered and not me, but I'll never know.

I'm never, ever, touching alcohol again.

* * *

I have a definite spring in my step as I walk home and it's not just because work is finished. Jack's not with me because he's gone to the gym so I have peace and quiet to mull over the events of the day.

I had a very long chat with Damien this afternoon.

I popped into his office to show him the results of my finished project and he was very complimentary about it and said that he'd make sure that the new manager knew how hard I'd worked on it. I felt really good when he said that, and also relieved, I just hope the new boss is as nice as Damien.

But that's not why I'm so happy.

I think Damien likes me; I mean, *likes* me.

When we've chatted over the last few weeks I've found out that he's single and not seeing anyone at the moment and without being too obvious, I've let him know that I'm single, too. Today, he asked me if I was going to his leaving drinks at the pub on Friday and when I said yes, he said that he was pleased to hear it and looked forward to seeing me there. There was a bit of a moment then, we looked at each other and didn't say anything and there was a definite hint of *something* in the air and I could feel myself blushing. I'm sure he went a bit red too, or perhaps I'm imagining it. So although I don't want to get carried away with myself, now he's not going to be my boss anymore, who knows what could happen? He already has my mobile number – as he has everyone else's in the department – so even when he's gone he can still contact me if he wants to.

I can't stop smiling to myself as I walk back to the flat because suddenly life feels full of opportunity; maybe my luck's about to change because let's face it, it's about time.

I let myself in and go into my bedroom and get changed into trackie bottoms and a t-shirt and think about what I'm going to have for dinner. My go-to is pasta because it's cheap and easy and I decide that's what it'll be tonight, too. Jack seems to live on takeaways of various sorts and he's lucky, because he never puts an ounce of weight on whereas I do, if I'm not careful. Also, it gets a bit expensive, and I'm trying to save money. I know by the time he gets back from the gym he'll want to order food but if I eat before he gets back I won't be tempted.

I put the kettle to boil and get my pasta out of the cupboard and throw some in a saucepan then sit down at the table and open up Facebook. Without thinking, I log onto my fake account and scroll to Rafe's feed. I do this on a daily basis and I don't know why. I'm almost certain that I don't care about him anymore but I can't seem to stop myself from seeing what's going on in his life and torturing myself with how fabulous his life looks compared to mine.

At first, I can't make sense of the picture that he's posted because it's blurry and in black and white, not colour. As it comes into focus, I see what it is and a hollow feeling floods through me and I wonder if I really am over him or if I'm just fooling myself. I read the text underneath the picture, although I don't really need to as I now realise that the black and white post is actually an ultrasound picture.

Rafe and Jacinta, it says, are thrilled to announce that they're twelve weeks pregnant with their first child.

CHAPTER SEVENTEEN

It was a shock.

Not least because it meant that she was already pregnant when they got married. For a brief moment, I tried to persuade myself that Rafe was forced to marry her and that he didn't love her, the same as he didn't love me, and that somehow that made me not such a failure.

But that's just utter nonsense, because they had a big, flash, posh wedding that they'd been planning for months and months because every sickening detail of it was all over Facebook.

Which means that the baby must have been planned.

I'm not going to lie it hurt when I saw that scan picture. Not because I want a baby, not yet anyway, but because it confirmed that Rafe never took me seriously at all. I was just a prolonged fling, alright for a bit of fun, useful for sex and house-cleaning and being the butt of his pathetic jokes. A stop-gap until the right woman came along.

No one wants to be thought of like that, do they?

But by the time I'd thought it through properly and calmed down, I realised that I didn't actually care very much, aside from my injured pride. Whilst I definitely don't wish them well – because I'm really not *that* nice – I don't wish Rafe dead anymore. I felt so sure of my non-feelings for him that I *almost* deleted my fake profile, but then stopped myself because I wanted to show the post to Jack so we could bitch about it together. Which I did the minute he got home from the gym and then instantly regretted, because now Jack knows that I still have a fake Facebook profile so I can look at Rafe's posts even though I told him I wasn't looking anymore. Jack never said anything but I could see him looking at me with a funny expression on his face and now I feel like a sad, deranged stalker who can't let go of the past.

Or maybe I imagined his expression, who knows. Anyway, I'll delete my fake profile soon. Probably.

Anyway, I'm definitely over Rafe and I think I might not bother with men at all for a long time. Not even Damien; I think I might have been imagining that he liked me, or maybe it was wishful thinking because nothing has happened since our meaningful look. The entire department went to the pub last night for his leaving drinks and it was a bit of an anti-climax. I hardly got to speak to Damien because there were so many people there and actually, what was I expecting? Darla and Pepe practically glued themselves to his side and completely monopolised him and no one else could get a look-in. Jack took full advantage of the free bar and drank pint after pint until he was swaying, whilst I stuck to one solitary orange juice and had a pretty boring time. Jack kept trying to persuade me just to have *just one drink* but I wasn't even tempted because I'm *never* drinking again.

Okay, maybe I was tempted a bit, because like I said, it was boring, but the main thing is, I didn't give in.

We left the pub just before nine because people had started to drift away by then and Damien announced loudly that he'd enjoyed working with us all and that'd he miss us.

And that was it.

Honestly, what was I expecting?

I am pathetic.

We came back to the flat and Jack went straight to bed and I sat and watched TV mindlessly until I felt tired enough to sleep, which turned out to be nearly one o'clock. It felt as if I'd only shut my eyes when the sound of the vacuum cleaner woke. When I looked at my phone I was shocked to see that it was eight-thirty.

Eight-thirty.

Who the fuck vacuums their flat at eight-thirty on a Saturday morning?

Jack does.

But worse was to come.

When I wandered out of my room and into the kitchen, bleary-eyed and desperate for a coffee, he turned the vacuum cleaner off and followed me. He told me that my jobs were to clean the kitchen worktops and wipe the cupboards down while he would clean the fridge out and mop the kitchen floor. He'd done the dusting, he said, although strictly speaking that was my job as he'd vacuumed the hallway and lounge but as it was my first week he'd let me off.

Honestly, I thought he was joking and I was waiting for the punch line but it never came. When it dawned on me that he was serious, I told him that I'd clean the kitchen just as soon as I'd had some breakfast and got dressed. He did the frowning thing again and I ignored him and made myself some toast but the atmosphere, well, you could cut it with a knife.

A clean one, obviously.

So after I was showered and dressed I cleaned the kitchen, which didn't actually need cleaning at all because it was pretty near spotless anyway. I could hear Jack in his bedroom vacuuming furiously and consoled myself with the fact that although I might feel forced into doing it, it wasn't actually hard work. I'd just finished when I heard the vacuum fall silent and Jack came back into the kitchen, all smiles.

'Glad that's all done for another week,' he said.

'Do you want me to put the vacuum cleaner in your bedroom?'

I looked at him blankly for a moment, because I didn't have a clue what he was talking about and then it gradually sank in.

'Okay, just leave it outside the door,' I said, because no way did I want him nosing in my room.

He trotted off and I heard him dragging the vacuum along the hallway so I gave it a few minutes and then went back to my room and dragged the vacuum inside. I closed the door, plugged the vacuum cleaner in, turned it on and then laid on my bed for ten minutes and scrolled through my phone.

Another one of my faults.

Treat me like a child and I'll behave like one.

I'm not proud of it, but there it is.

* * *

Jack's gone out for the night.

He was all dressed up his finest and splashed with a good dose of aftershave and he did look good, he had just the right amount of stubble and his blonde hair looked lush because he has the sort of hair that always looks good even if he's just climbed out of bed. His eyes were all twinkly, his shirt enhanced his biceps and he looked super-hot. As I studied him, I asked myself why I don't fancy him and I couldn't find an answer; he's hot, funny and a nice guy, if a bit over the top about cleaning. He's not quite as hot as Rafe but Jack's a looker, there's no doubt about that but you can't fake chemistry; it's either there or it's not.

Once he'd gone it felt nice to have the place to myself and I'm treating myself to a pamper night and some trash TV. I've given my face a good buffing with an expensive face cloth that I bought ages ago and it looks all shiny and clean. Next I'm going to paint my toenails a brilliant red.

I've decided that next Saturday night I'm not going to be a sad loser spending her evening on her own, I'm going to join my workmates on their weekly night out. Every Friday an email goes around the whole department asking who's up for a night out. There's a hardcore pack of around ten who *always* go but everyone is welcome and if you're on your own it's an opportunity for a night out where you won't feel like a spare part. I've only been a few times; when I first started in the office I still had other friends that I used to go out with and then when I met Rafe, I never went out except with him. After we finished, I went out a couple of times with the guys from the office but would disappear once we were in a club. I'd then drink myself into a stupor.

I won't be doing that this time.

I put my feet up on the coffee table and undo the top of the bottle of nail varnish and give my nails a first coat. Not that anyone will be seeing them because it's nearly November and I'm hardly going to be wearing strappy sandals, but for some reason, painted toenails always make me feel good.

I let them dry and then give them another coat and am attempting to put the top on the bottle when the brush falls out of my hands and bounces onto the carpet. I quickly pick it up but it's too late, there's a scarlet stripe of nail polish on the floor. I stare down at it in horror and imagine Jack's face. Pulling a wet wipe out of the packet I attempt to wipe it off the carpet but it does nothing. Determined not to panic, I Google it. Google tells me to spray it with hairspray and then splash some drops of nail polish remover onto it and scrub it with a small brush.

I leap off the sofa and practically run to my bedroom and through into the bathroom and grab the can of hairspray from the shelf. I hurry back out into the lounge and stare at the carpet and tell myself not to panic. I put the hairspray next to the nail polish remover on the table and go out into the kitchen. I need a small brush; I stare around the kitchen looking for inspiration, there must be a scrubbing brush somewhere in this kitchen because Jack is bound to have one because he's always cleaning.

I look in the cupboard underneath the sink but aside from assorted cleaning products and a bucket, there's nothing. I sit back on my heels and think and then reach behind all of the stuff and pull the bucket out. The bucket's full of bits and pieces and I pull out a handful of cleaning cloths, a large sponge, a small scrubbing brush and a random stray button. Everything smells strongly of bleach and I start to think that maybe Jack's not a neat freak, maybe he has a bit of an obsession. Not that it matters now, I need to get the nail polish off that carpet.

I hurry back into the lounge and crouch down on the floor and following the instructions from my internet search to the letter, I attempt to remove the stain.

Half-an-hour later, I sit back and stare at the carpet. It looks okay, I can't see any hint of red and I think maybe I need to stop now before I start rubbing the pile of the carpet away. I take the scrubbing brush out to the kitchen and rinse it under the tap and then put it back in the bucket in the kitchen cupboard and replace it exactly as I found it. I go back into the lounge and sit at various points on each of the sofas to stare at the carpet to see if I there's a stain. I can't see anything. Jack will have no idea what's happened unless he gets down on the floor with a magnifying glass.

I take my nail polishes and clutter back into my bedroom and put it all away and then recheck the lounge to make sure that I haven't left anything in there. I then turn the lights off in the lounge and go into my room. Jack probably won't be back for hours because he's clubbing, which is good because I don't want to see him tonight because I'll have guilt written all over my face. It's only ten-thirty but I feel surprisingly tired. This is payback for pretending to vacuum my bedroom this afternoon.

After brushing my teeth I climb into bed and turn out the light and fall almost immediately into a deep sleep.

* * *

I awake with a start. I've been dreaming; disjointed snatches of weird dreams that usually only happens when I've been binge drinking. I try to recall what the dreams were but they drift away like smoke from a chimney and I'm left with the distinct feeling that I'm missing something important.

A loud moan from the other side of the bedroom wall startles me and I catch my breath and wonder what the hell's happening. I then hear the unmistakable sound of a woman panting noisily and I realise that Jack is home and he's brought someone with him. I lie silently and listen as the moaning becomes louder and the woman's moans turn to loud gasps of *oh God* and I cover my ears so I don't have to listen to them both reaching orgasm.

When I'm sure that it must all be over, I slowly uncover my ears. Thankfully, the moaning has stopped and has been replaced by the low murmur of voices and a woman's laughter. I wonder if the woman will still be here in the morning and if I'm going to have to make polite conversation with her over the breakfast table. I wonder whether Jack will cook her breakfast.

Just like he did for me.
Awkward or what.

CHAPTER EIGHTEEN

I never usually get up early on a Sunday morning, but by eight o'clock I was in the shower washing my hair.

The sounds of Jack and the woman he brought home with him last night woke me again at ten-to-eight and after ten minutes I couldn't stand it any longer so I got up. By the time I've dried my hair and got dressed the noises have stopped.

I wonder if she's gone.

Or maybe she's in the kitchen having breakfast with Jack.

I sit on the bed for a while and debate staying in my room until I'm certain she's not here. Am I going to do this every time he has someone stay the night? If I do, it's saying that a woman he's brought home for the night has more right to be in this flat than me. I'm paying rent for this, I tell myself, and I'm not going to be embarrassed to be in my own home. I take a deep breath, open my bedroom door and walk out into the hallway and walk straight through into the kitchen before I can change my mind.

Jack is standing at the cooker in his boxers stirring what looks like a pan of scrambled eggs. The boxers are skin tight and leave nothing to the imagination.

'Morning.' He beams a wide smile at me, looking up as I walk in.

'Morning,' I say, walking over to the kettle. I pick it up and take it to the sink and fill it from the tap, trying not to look at the girl sitting at the kitchen table.

'This is my flatmate, Josie,' Jack says, walking across to the girl and putting his hand on her shoulder.

'Hi,' I say, with a smile in her direction. She's young, much younger than Jack, much younger than me. She can't be much more than eighteen.

'Hi,' she says, with a hesitant smile which makes her look even younger. She's wearing the shirt that Jack had on last night and she tugs it down over her knees as she looks up at me. I watch as Jack squeezes her shoulder and then his hand drops slightly and he slides his fingers down the opening of the shirt. I look away and concentrate on getting a mug out of the cupboard.

'Jack!' I hear her giggle and sneak a glance out of the corner of my eye just in time to see her pulling

Jack's hand out of the shirt. Intent on treating the situation as if it's perfectly normal, I hold the jar up in the air.

'Anyone want coffee?' I ask.

'Yeah, I'll have one,' Jack says, before turning to the girl. 'How about you? Sorry, what's your name again? I've forgotten.'

Her face flushes scarlet and I can almost feel her humiliation as she answers.

'Brittany,' she says, quietly. 'And I really have to go now but thanks for the offer of the coffee.'

'But I've made you breakfast, *Brittany*.' Jack says, without smiling, saying her name as if he's making some sort of point. 'Aren't you going to eat it?'

'I, I really need to go,' she says, standing up.

Jack sighs loudly and shrugs and there's an awkward silence as she hurries out of the kitchen towards his bedroom.

'That was a bit much,' I say, quietly, when she's out of earshot.

'What?' Jack says, as he leans up against the counter and folds his arms.

'You. The way you treated her.'

'Don't know what you mean. Do you want this?' He points at the scrambled egg and when I shake my head he turns and switches the oven ring off and moves the saucepan off the heat.

'Not very gentlemanly,' I say. 'Not even remembering her name, you could have pretended you knew it.'

He shrugs again and laughs.

'Why? It was a one-night stand. A mutual night of sex with no strings attached. We're hardly in a relationship so what do I need to know her name for?'

'Good manners?' I pour boiling water onto the coffee in both mugs, slop milk into each and hand him one. He doesn't answer but sits down in the chair that Brittany's vacated and takes a noisy slurp from his coffee.

'Why don't you go and get dressed?' I ask.

'In a while,' he says.

'You could at least put some trousers on,' I say. 'Instead of sitting around in your boxers.'

'Why?' he looks down at himself. 'It's not like you haven't seen it before, is it?'

I don't say anything and I will my face not to flush.

'Although,' he says, with a smirk. 'You did a lot more than just look at it as I remember. A whole lot more and then some.'

I march along to my cupboard and open the door and pretend to rummage around for my bread. I wish I'd stayed in my room now and not come out because quite frankly, right now, I'd like to punch Jack right in the face, mate or no mate.

'I'm off now,' a small voice says from the kitchen doorway.

I close the cupboard door and turn to see a fully dressed Brittany. She's wearing a tight mini-skirt with a strappy top and she looks impossibly young and fragile.

'Haven't you got a coat?' I ask, sounding like my mother,

'Yeah,' she says, pulling a tiny blouson jacket on. 'I was going to call a cab but I haven't got your address?'

She looks at Jack hopefully but he ignores her and stares into his mug as he drinks his coffee.

'Jack?' I say, loudly. 'Can't you give Brittany a lift home? You know what it's like for getting a cab on a Sunday morning.'

'No can do.' He drains the last few drops of coffee and puts the mug on the table with a clatter. 'Still over the limit.'

He gets up from the table and saunters towards Brittany and she can't disguise the look of hope in her eyes as he gets closer. He doesn't look at her but eases himself through the door and around her as he goes and I see his hand snake downwards and squeeze her bottom as he goes.

'Gotta go back to bed,' he says, over his shoulder to no one in particular. 'Josie will give you the address.' And with that parting shot he saunters back to his bedroom and I hear the sound of his door closing.

I stare at Brittany and have a horrible feeling that she's going to cry; her bottom lip is quivering and she looks about twelve-years-old.

'I'll call you a cab,' I say. 'I know a good one who always turns up. I'll just go and get my phone.' I brush past her and go to my room and grab my phone and take it back into the kitchen. I can hear the sound of Jack's TV from his bedroom and it crosses my mind that he couldn't be more insulting if he tried.

I scroll through my contacts and call my go-to cab company and try to keep my temper in check.

Jack, mate, you're an absolute bastard.

* * *

Jack eventually came out of his room at about three o'clock in the afternoon. He was freshly showered and dressed and showed absolutely no sign of a hangover. He had his bed sheets bundled in his arms and he stuffed them into the washing machine, added liquid and put it on to wash. He then went out into the hallway, pulled the vacuum cleaner out of the cupboard and took it into his bedroom and turned it on.

Ten minutes later he dragged the vacuum out from his bedroom and shoved it back into the cupboard.

'She moulted like a bloody cat,' he says, pulling a face. 'Long, dark, hair everywhere.'

'Really?' I said, with disinterest as I put my coat on and buttoned it up. Whilst he'd been vacuuming, I'd made the decision that I needed to get out of the flat before I said something to him that I'd regret. I planned on going into town and looking around the shops for a few hours and hopefully by the time I got back, I'd feel in a better mood.

As I trudged around the shops I faced the fact that sharing a flat with Jack wasn't going to work. It wasn't just the fact of being woken up by their loud sex, it was more the way he treated Brittany. I saw a side to Jack that I don't like and if I carry on flat sharing with him, I can see myself falling out with him.

I know she was a one-night stand and it was only sex but I wonder if it was more than that for her. I might not remember actually having sex with Jack but I definitely remember the way he flattered me the next day. I totally believed what he said and I'm a grown woman and I didn't even *want* to believe him. If he did the same kind of thing to talk Brittany into bed, I can imagine her thinking that it actually meant something to him because she seemed so young and vulnerable. I think he used her and it doesn't sit well with me.

And that's another thing that shocked me; why choose someone so young? There are plenty of woman around Jack's own age who are always up for no-strings sex, so why pick on a young girl who to me, seemed quite innocent. And the way he cleaned his room after she'd gone felt weird, as if she'd tainted it. It made me wonder if he did that with me once I'd gone home.

I so wish that I'd never spent the night with Jack, because it's making me look at him in a different way and I don't like it. What exactly did he say to *me* to get me into bed? Because something made me do it.

The only options I have are to save quicker and faster for my mortgage deposit or move into a shared house elsewhere. Tired of tramping around the shops and determined not to buy things that I don't need, I go into Costa and order a coffee. I sit down at a window table and scroll through my phone, searching the spare room ads. There aren't many vacancies at all and the only ones available are miles from work and the rent is still more than I pay Jack. Most of them are sharing with at least three people and how will I feel if they're all into bringing people home to shag? At least I won't know them, I tell myself, so I won't care what they do. Maybe there'll be house rules about that sort of thing, who knows? Olivia and I never had the conversation about bringing guys home but if she had bought a man home, it would have felt different because she's another woman.

I give up scrolling when my phone battery dips to twenty-per-cent and I wonder how much a replacement battery would cost. It seems to run out of charge in no time at all lately and I don't use it *that* much. Maybe I've worn it out with all the snooping on Rafe's Facebook.

Serves me right.

I stare out of the window onto the High Street and try to think logically and without emotion. If only Olivia hadn't decided that I was the devil incarnate I could still be living there. She wasn't the greatest but now I realise that she wasn't *that* bad, despite her bat shit crazy fantasies about me going into her bedroom.

I put my phone in my bag and take a last sip of my cold coffee. People are waiting for tables and I don't think I can sit here any longer unless I buy another drink and I don't want to spend money on a coffee that I don't want. I push the chair back and get up and a young couple immediately swoop in and claim my table. I walk out onto the High Street and face the fact that I'll have to stay at Jack's. I'll just have to get on with it and make the most of it. If Jack is having a girl stay over every weekend, I'm going to stay in my room the next day until she's gone and put the TV on loud so that I can't hear them. Going by today's events, they're hardly encouraged to stay around for very long. I'll buy some earplugs to wear on a Saturday night so I don't have to listen to him shagging.

I start to walk home and my stomach rumbles and I remember I haven't eaten anything since breakfast and it's now nearly four o'clock. There's only work to look forward to tomorrow and I think that, realistically, I need to start properly applying for other jobs in the company. Aside from advancing my career, living and working with Jack is going to be too much, I need to broaden my horizons. My phone bleeps and as I dip my hand into my handbag and pull it out, I guess that it's Jack, wondering where I am. He'll be ready to order his usual Sunday night pizza and wanting to know if I'm going to share it with him.

I tap the screen to see a WhatsApp notification

and I stare at it for a moment, trying to make sense of it.

It's not Jack.

It's Damien.

CHAPTER NINETEEN

This week has dragged and seems to have lasted forever but at last it's Friday and there's only one more night to go.

One more night before my date with Damien.

His WhatsApp message came in at exactly the right time; there I was feeling totally dejected and pissed off with Jack and imagining every Saturday being the same when *boom*, Damien messages me. I'd become convinced that I'd imagined that spark between us but it turns out that I haven't. I don't need to look at my phone to remind myself what the message says because I've memorised it. *Hey Josie, how are you? Sorry I didn't get an opportunity to speak to you on Friday night but I was wondering if you'd like to meet for dinner one evening?*

I stood in the doorway of the coffee shop and was about to message him right back but then stopped myself. I'd wait until I got back to the flat to reply, because I didn't want to look completely desperate. The minute I got back to the flat I went into my bedroom and replied to his message. We had a bit of WhatsApp back and forth and eventually agreed on dinner for Saturday night. We're meeting at a restaurant in town that Damien often goes to and he's booked a table for eight o'clock. Damien offered to pick me up from the flat but I said that I'd meet him at the restaurant.

Because I haven't yet told Jack that I have a date with Damien.

I honestly *was* going to tell him but I know that he's going to sneer about it because he doesn't like Damien and I don't want my date spoiled by him keeping on about it. I know Jack; he'll be dropping snide comments all week and I'll have to constantly bite my tongue or alternatively, have a huge row with him. I can't be bothered. It's just one date. If it develops into something, of course I'll tell him but for now, he doesn't need to know, he's just a mate, not my mother.

As far as Jack's concerned, I'm going out with the crowd from the office on Saturday because that's all he needs to know. We're back to our easy, friends' relationship and he hasn't mentioned Brittany and nor have I. I saw a side to Jack that I don't like but I'm not going to question him about his behaviour or the way he treats women because it's nothing to do with me. Neither of us are perfect and Jack's never judged me for me for my binge drinking so I can hardly judge him for the way he treats women.

I have bought myself a new dress, even though I'm saving, because I think a date with a new man deserves a new dress. It's nothing flash; just a smart black number that'll look classy with a pair of heels. Every time I think about Saturday night I get butterflies. I think I must have regressed to being a teenager, although as this is my first date since Rafe, I think I can be forgiven.

Apart from the night with Jack.

But that was a big mistake and I'm over that now and we're back to being mates, although I did have a strange conversation with Darla earlier in the week. I was at the mini-kitchen on Wednesday lunchtime making myself a coffee and Darla came over to make herself some toast and we started chatting. She can talk for England and is the office gossip and I wasn't really listening, if I'm honest, but when she said that she was going on the office night out I had to lie and say that I was going too. Obviously I'm not, I just won't turn up and no one will notice and by Monday morning it'll all be forgotten. She laughed when I said I was going and made a weird comment about *Jack not liking it*. I looked at her and asked her what she meant and she did her typical Darla-thing and covered her mouth with her hand and said *oops*.

She always does that, because she wants you to coax the gossip out of her to make her feel important. I don't normally bother because I find it annoying and it's usually non-news or totally made-up but as the comment was about Jack, I thought I'd better make the effort.

'What do you mean, Jack won't like it?' I asked. 'What's me going out got to do with him?'

'Well, you know,' she said, all coy. 'You two are living together now, aren't you?'

'We're *flat-sharing*,' I said, with a laugh. 'That's all.'

'Oh, okay,' she said, with a fake shrug, resuming buttering her toast, which I knew meant I was supposed to beg her to tell me. I was so tempted not to bother because she's just a gossip and always gets stuff completely wrong or makes it up, but I couldn't help myself because curiosity got the better of me.

'Come on, Darla,' I said. 'You can't say something leading like that and then just clam up. Spill.'

'Well.' The butter knife went down again and her toast must have been stone cold by then. 'I'm not supposed to say anything but *everyone* knows that Jack has the hots for you.'

I couldn't help laughing and she looked all offended then and said that she wasn't making it up and she wished she hadn't told me now. I asked her where she'd got the idea he had the hots for me from and she did her coy thing and said she *never reveals her sources*. Which means she made it up. I told her that I'd tell Jack what she'd said because he'd have a good laugh about it too. Her face dropped and she was suddenly serious and said, *please don't, because you know how he hates being gossiped about.* And I knew then that Darla must have been on the receiving end of one of Jack's moods to react like that. I was almost tempted to tell him so she'd think twice about spreading gossip in the future.

But I didn't, because it wouldn't stop her and there's no harm in her really, and maybe our conversation would make her think twice in the future. I don't really care what gossip there is about me in the office because I'd rather harmless stuff like that goes around than the real stuff like crashing weddings and having a go at my now dead boss. I could have told her about Brittany and all the other women that Jack shags and that would have quelled the rumours about me and him. But I didn't bother; let people think what they like because they will anyway.

If Damien and I become a thing, the rumour mill will be spinning like a top and then Darla really will have something to talk about.

And actually, I have a good feeling about Damien.

I can't wait for tomorrow night.

* * *

I arrive at the restaurant with minutes to spare and as I walk in, I'm relieved to see that Damien is already seated at a table near the window that looks out onto the High Street. I'm not going to be stood up. Did I really think that he'd not turn up? There was a bit of doubt in my mind and I think it's because I can't quite believe my luck. Damien must have been looking out for me because he stands up and waves and after a nod at the maitre d', I make my way across the restaurant towards him.

I'm glad I made the effort with my appearance because the closer I get, the more gorgeous he looks. He always looked gorgeous, even at work, because it's not possible for someone as good-looking as him to look anything else. Although, if he had appalling dress sense he wouldn't look *quite* so hot, but tonight he looks as impeccably dressed as he always does. He's not wearing a tie, because he's not at work, and his shirt has the top two buttons undone and his trousers and jacket are casual, yet smart. I congratulate myself on my new dress because I know I look good and my hair, unusually, also looks good instead of refusing to do as it's told.

'Hi,' he says, leaning to kiss me on the check as I arrive at the table. 'Good to see you.'

'You too,' I say, taking in the hint of an aroma of his citrus aftershave.

A waiter has silently appeared at the table and after taking my coat he pulls out the chair for me and I sit down.

'I thought we'd start with some bubbles, is that okay?' Damien looks at me with a questioning look.

'Perfect,' I say.

The waiter reappears and proceeds to uncork a bottle of champagne and pour us both a glass. I can't help feeling impressed; no one has ever bought me champagne before and somehow, even though Rafe was the rich one, I mostly ended up paying for him. When the waiter has gone, Damien picks up his glass and holds it in the air.

'To a good evening,' he says, softly.

I pick my flute up and we chink glasses and I take the tiniest of sips. I can't refuse to drink it, can I? I know I'm off alcohol but it'll just look weird if I tell him that now. It would spoil the moment. Vowing never to drink again is all very well but it's a lot easier said than done.

'You look stunning tonight,' he says, staring into my eyes.

'Thank you,' I say, taking a gulp of champagne, despite my promise to myself. It's practically fizzy pop anyway, hardly alcohol at all.

'So, how have you been, Josie? I've missed our daily chats.'

'Me too,' I say, putting my glass down on the table to stop myself from guzzling it all. 'How is it back in the financial world?'

'Oh, you know,' he says, with a wave of his hand. 'Pretty dull without you to chat to, if I'm honest.'

'Flatterer,' I say, with a laugh.

He smiles and his eyes twinkle and I want to pinch myself to make sure that I'm really here and I'm not dreaming.

'To be honest, this dating thing is quite new to

me.' He smiles ruefully. 'I've just come out of a long relationship and I feel like the new boy. Everything has changed so much from when I last took anyone out for dinner.'

'Oh, sorry to hear that. About your relationship, I mean.'

'Don't be,' he says, picking up his glass and taking a sip. 'I'm not. The relationship lingered on for far longer than it should have done and now I'm looking to the future.'

'Actually.' I pick up my glass to give myself some courage. 'I've not long come out of a long relationship myself so I know how you feel.'

A bit of a lie as it was over a year ago but Damien doesn't need to know that. The feelings are the same.

'Really? Wow, fancy that.' He smiles. 'So you know exactly how I feel.'

'I do.' I take another sip of champagne.

'Don't you think,' he says, opening the menu. 'That's there's so much you've been missing out on? I mean, tying yourself down to one person for years? I know I do.'

'Definitely,' I agree, although I'm not really sure what he means.

'You know, doing the same things all the time, the same old routine. I don't want that anymore, I want excitement, new horizons and all that.'

'Me too.' I put the glass down and realise that it's empty. Slow down, Josie, don't ruin this night.

'So, what would you like to eat?'

I pick the menu up and stare at it unseeingly. It's in French and there are no translations and my language skills are rusty, to say the least. Not that they were very good to start with.

I pretend to read the menu as Damien pours more champagne into my glass. I don't stop him.

''How about.' I fold the menu closed and place it on the table. 'You order for me. See if you can guess what I like?'

He grins and I relax; he probably orders for his dates all of the time. As long as he doesn't order snails, I'll be fine. Although I'd probably eat them if he did because I'm so desperate to impress him.

The waiter appears at our table and Damien reels off our order in fluent French and I have no idea what he's saying. I look out of the window and watch the usual Saturday pub and club-goers as groups of them wander in and out of the pub opposite. The majority of the pubs are in the old town and my work-mates will have started the night off in The Kings Arms already. I wonder if one of them will mention my non-attendance in work next week and what I'll say if Jack overhears. I should have just told him instead of lying, I don't need his approval about who I date. I didn't approve of him bringing Brittany home and he didn't give a shit.

As I stare out of the window, I catch a glimpse of the back of a man's head as he stands in a shop doorway lighting a cigarette and there's something so familiar about him that for a moment, I think that it's Jack. I smile to myself at my own guilty conscience and take another sip of champagne and when I look again, the man is gone.

'All ordered,' Damien says. 'I hope you like it.'

'Oh, I will,' I say. 'I'm sure you've got very good taste.'

Damien smiles warmly and I smile back.

A vision pops into my head; when Jack gets up tomorrow morning he encounters me cooking Damien breakfast in the kitchen. I can't help smiling at the thought of the look on Jack's face.

'Something funny?' Damien asks, with a raised eyebrow.

'Oh, nothing much,' I lie. 'I was just thinking if my flatmate was here. He hates French food, this would be his worst nightmare.'

Damien reaches across the table and takes my hand.

'Well,' he says, stroking my fingers. 'It's fortunate he's not joining us.'

I don't tell him it's Jack, and that he knows him, because I don't want to talk about anyone else. I concentrate on the feeling of my hand in Damien's and wish that this night would never end.

CHAPTER TWENTY

As I attempt to clamber out of Damien's car as elegantly as I can, I spot the familiar figure of Jack standing on the balcony smoking a cigarette. He may be six floors up but there's no doubt in my mind that he'll have seen me because he doesn't miss a thing. I wonder if he had a girl stay over last night; if he has, with a bit of luck she'll be gone by now because it's nearly lunchtime.

I lean in to the car and say goodbye to Damien and he smiles and says he'll call me. I close the car door and stand and wave as he zooms off. I make my way towards the flats' entrance, looking up and waving to Jack as I go. He doesn't wave back and I think that maybe he hasn't seen me after all. If he hasn't, am I going to lie about where I've been or just tell him the truth and get his snide comments about Damien over with?

I'll decide when I see him, because for now, I just want to savour the memory of last night. I didn't intend going back to Damien's flat and spending the night with him but it just sort of happened. I wasn't drunk; I drank three glasses of champagne and felt slightly tipsy but I definitely wasn't drunk and I remember every minute of it, no blackouts at all.

Although actually, now I think about it, maybe I had more than three glasses as Damien only had one glass because he was driving. Not that it matters, I was fine.

We had a wonderful night; the only thing that slightly marred it was when he started talking about Evelyn and how terrible it all was and wondering if we'd ever know what happened to her. I made the right noises in the right places but I was glad when the conversation moved on because I didn't want to talk about her. I don't want to be reminded of her or her nastiness or our meeting on the night she was murdered.

I was slightly relieved when our meals arrived and I discovered that Damien had ordered pate to start followed by chicken in a delicious lemon sauce. I would have eaten anything but was pleased it wasn't frog's legs or snails. The portions may have been tiny but the food was outstanding. As we were lingering over our coffee after we'd finished our dessert, Damien took hold of my hand again and told me how he felt that he'd known me for much longer than a few weeks and wasn't it strange how you could feel so close to someone so quickly? We gazed into each other's eyes and it felt like the best night of my life.

He wouldn't even let me pay – and I know that restaurant is ridiculously expensive – and told me not to insist as it would spoil the night. When he suggested a nightcap at his place as he lived nearby I didn't refuse – although I never did drink the brandy he poured me. And although I don't normally sleep with a guy on a first date – apart from Rafe, who was different – it didn't feel tacky at all. Damien was attentive and sweet and everything he should be and I really feel this could be the start of something good.

We just clicked and we talked and talked and talked, about everything – obviously not about Rafe because the less said about him, the better – but everything else. His ex was the jealous type and he said that he never realised how much she restricted his life until he was free of her. And *she* dumped *him*; how could any woman in her right mind dump Damien? And doesn't the fact that he told me he was dumped say something good about him? Because what guy wants to admit they've been ditched? Not many, if any.

Right now I'm on cloud nine and if Jack is the mate that I think he is, he's going to be so happy for me, so pleased that I've found someone good at last.

The events of last night are going through my

mind as I let myself into the flat and it's feels like an anti-climax when I'm met by silence. There's no noise or chatter so if Jack did bring someone home last night, they're not here now. It's unusually quiet, because Jack nearly always has the TV on even when he's not watching it but there's nothing, no sound at all.

'Hi,' I call out, walking into the lounge. The balcony doors are wide open and the cold air is rushing in but there's no sign of Jack. The sight of the open doors makes me feel nervous but I can't bring myself to walk over and close them. My fear of heights conjures up a vision of me walking to close the doors and tripping on the step and falling over the balcony and plummeting to the car park below.

Ridiculous, I know, but I can't go near the doors, nevertheless. I walk out into the kitchen and nearly jump out of my skin when I see Jack sitting silently at the kitchen table.

'Christ, Jack, you nearly gave me a heart attack.'

He looks up at me unsmilingly and then resumes studying his phone.

'You've left the balcony doors open,' I say.

'Well, close them, then,' he says, without looking up.

He knows very well that I can't so I turn to leave the kitchen. He's obviously in a right mood and I can't even be bothered to talk to him. As I go into the hall his voice stops me.

'You could have let me know you weren't

coming home.'

I swivel on my heels and stare at him.

'What?'

'You could have let me know you were staying out all night.'

'Why would I let you know?' I demand. 'You're not my mother.'

'No, I'm your *friend*,' Jack says. 'And I was worried. A simple text would have done.'

Should I have let him know? I try to imagine if he'd stayed out all night, would I expect him to let me know? I wouldn't; I honestly wouldn't expect him to tell me.

'My phone was dead, otherwise I would have done.' The part about my phone being dead is true, saying I would have texted him is a lie but it seems easier than arguing about something so stupid.

'So where were you?' Jack asks.

'With a friend,' I say.

'Would that be the friend who just dropped you off?'

'It would.'

He sniffs and resumes scrolling on his phone. Did he know it was Damien or was he too far away to see? Six stories up is a long way. I only knew it was Jack on the balcony because I know which flat is ours and it's on the corner.

'You could have texted me on your friend's phone,' he says, as I'm about to give up trying to talk to him and go to my bedroom.

'Really?' I say. 'I have to check in and out now, do

I? Even when I lived with Olivia I never had to do that and she was a complete nutjob.'

'Oh, I'm sorry,' Jack says, sarcastically. '*Sorry* I care about where you are and if you've been murdered. *Sorry* I'm being a proper friend.'

'Okay,' I say, equally sarcastically. 'You bring girls back here and shag them but how do I know you haven't brought some bat-shit crazy psycho back with you who's going to murder us in our beds? You're hardly sensible, are you, so don't come over all high and mighty with me.'

'That's different,' he says. 'I'm a man.'

I gawp at him as I realise that he's actually serious. Time to wind this conversation up and retreat to my bedroom before I say something I'll regret.

'I appreciate your concern.' I say, calmly. 'But honestly, you've absolutely no need to worry about me, I'm fine.'

'You're not though, are you?' he snorts. 'Because you binge drink until you're practically unconscious and then can't remember anything that you've done or where you've been. How am I supposed to know you're alright? Have you forgotten our bitch of a boss was murdered a matter of weeks ago and they still haven't caught who did it? Actually, Josie, you're fucking selfish and I'm shocked at how much you don't fucking care after all I've done for you.'

I stare at him in shock.

'I never thought about you worrying like that,'

I manage to say. 'It honestly never crossed my mind.'

He stares at me for a moment without speaking and then there's the hint of a smile and for a moment, the old Jack is back in the room.

'It's alright,' he says, eventually. 'Just think next time, okay?'

I nod and stretch my lips into the semblance of a smile but inside I'm raging. How dare he talk to me as if I'm a child. I want to shout at him and tell him what an absolute chauvinistic pig he is and tell him exactly what I think of him, but I don't. This is an argument that I'm not going to win and I need to placate him because I'm living in his flat and have nowhere else to go.

But not for long, I suddenly realise.

I'm going to find somewhere else to live as soon as possible. I don't want to live with a controlling friend who has one rule for him and another for me. And actually, what has he done for me? Yeah, I'm sharing his flat but it was hardly a selfless gesture, was it? He needed a flatmate and I needed somewhere to live so he hasn't actually done anything for me. Sadly, I now realise that it's true that you don't really know someone until you live with them because I've never seen this side of Jack before. I need to get away from him now before I say something that's going to make it impossible to live here.

'Jack,' I say, turning to go to my bedroom. 'Do you think you could shut the balcony doors? It's blowing a gale in there and you know how nervous I feel when they're open.'

He sighs and puts his phone down on the table and stands up.

'Okay,' he says. 'I'll close them.'

I go out into the hallway and head towards my bedroom and watch as he follows me down the hallway, turns into the lounge and goes over to the balcony doors and pulls them shut. He locks them with the key that's in the lock, twists the handle to show me they're shut and looks at me.

'Happy, now?' he asks.

'Yes, thank you.'

'No problem.' He crosses the room and flops onto the sofa, picks up the remote control and turns on the TV. I go into my bedroom and close the door and ask myself; did he leave the doors open on purpose just to unsettle me?

I think he did.

* * *

After I've showered and dressed, I spend the afternoon catching up on my washing and ironing. As I'm hanging the wet washing over the clothes rack in my bedroom it strikes me that there are quite a few house-rules that I have to adhere to.

Wet washing; Jack won't tolerate clothes drying on radiators or clothes racks anywhere in the flat, it has to be out of sight in my own room. He says washing makes the place look like a Chinese laundry and he can't stand it. He informed me of this the first time I attempted to put some of my jumpers on a rail over the hall radiator, and it was accompanied by his trademark frown. He dries all of his stuff in the tumble dryer he said, so why didn't I do the same.

Because some stuff would come out shrunken beyond belief, that's why, Jack, because unlike you, I have some delicate stuff that I'd quite like to keep wearing. I can't leave so much as a crumb on the worktop, let alone a cup or a knife, and while I can tolerate this, what I can't tolerate is him thinking he has some sort of right to comment on my life or expect me to inform him where I am. I'm going to have to keep the peace while I look for somewhere else but as soon as possible, I'll be gone.

Olivia doesn't seem quite so bad now.

After I've finished my washing and ironing, I set about cleaning my bathroom and bedroom. I don't really want to do it, but equally, I don't want to sit in the lounge with Jack. I'll have to, obviously, because I'll have to try and get over the awkwardness, but I'm not looking forward to it and that makes me feel sad because he's my friend and I don't like feeling that way about him.

Which is why I need to move out quickly and then we can be proper mates again. I don't want to end up hating him.

I finish vacuuming my room and drag the cleaner back out into the hallway and put it in the cupboard.

I can't put it off any longer.
Time to sit in the lounge with Jack.

* * *

It wasn't so bad; I kept the conversation light and general – no mention of Damien – and neither of us referred to our previous spat. I even shared his Sunday night takeaway pizza with him. But it didn't make me change my mind; I am going to find somewhere else to live as quickly as possible.

I was a bit disappointed that I didn't hear from Damien, but then I reminded myself that I only saw him earlier so he has no need to text me today. To be honest, the spat with Jack has taken the shine off my night with Damien. I can't bring myself to tell Jack about Damien because I know he'll slag him off endlessly and I'll end up defending him and we'll have a proper row then.

When it got to ten o'clock I got up from the sofa and said I was going to bed. This wasn't totally unusual for me as I often have an early night but Jack did that frowning thing again and for a minute I felt like slapping him.

I *did* go straight to bed, because it wasn't a lie, I was tired, but I can't say I slept very well. I tossed and turned to get to sleep, running the row with Jack over in my mind and when I fell asleep it wasn't restful. I woke up hot, sweaty and agitated and when I looked at my phone it was just gone four o'clock in the morning. I'd somehow managed to wrap myself up in a cocoon of my quilt so I must have been thrashing around in some sort of nightmare.

Disturbed sleep isn't unusual for me, although it usually only happens after I've been drinking. Nightmares are not unusual, either, although I never remember them properly, only snippets.

I couldn't remember this one, either.

But I did remember something else; something that has been lurking at the back of my mind since last week and when I remembered, the significance of it hit me and I never slept anymore but lay awake until I got up at seven o'clock.

Because, truthfully, what I'd remembered frightened me.

CHAPTER TWENTY-ONE

I rang in sick this morning, on a Monday, which is probably the very worst day that you call pull a sickie because it looks so obvious.

But I don't care.

I told our new temporary manager, Donald, that I thought I had the flu and he answered with the usual *do you think you'll be in tomorrow* and I said I'd see how I feel. I think it must be company policy to ask that question but they should change it because it's stupid; how am I supposed to know how I'm going to feel in twenty-four hours time?

I told Jack the same lie. I even affected a little cough and made sure I looked a right mess with my hair all over the place to emphasise how ill I was. I *think* he believed me, although he did do the frowning thing as if he didn't approve, so I'm not totally sure. The frown was a bloody cheek considering the numerous fictitious doctor and dentist appointments that he's always skiving off work for. Although it doesn't really matter if he believes me, he's just left the flat to go work and that's all that I care about, that he's gone.

Because I have to search his room.

I have no idea what I'm looking for but Jack has been up to something, and I need to find out what. The thing that I remembered in the early hours of the morning was the button.

The button that I found in the bucket underneath the sink.

I know that button.

It's quite distinctive; it's made of brass or some sort of gold covered metal, and it has a slightly military looking design to it although it's not from a military coat.

It's from the coat that I lost on the night of Rafe's wedding.

What is Jack doing with it? Where did he get it and how did it end up in a bucket underneath his sink?

I've tried to convince myself that it must have fallen off my coat when I've visited Jack but I know that's not the case. That coat had all of its buttons on the day of Rafe's wedding because when I left Olivia's flat, I did the coat up. It was cold outside and the white dress I was wearing was made of thin material and not warm at all.

Which means that Jack must have seen me on that day.

So why hasn't he told me?

Did I come here, in those lost hours?

And if I did, why did I wake up late that night on a park bench?

None of it makes any sense but what I do know is that I don't trust Jack anymore and I need to find out what he's hiding from me. I think he knows something about that night and I need him to tell me, even if it's something that I don't want to hear. I need to find something to *make* him tell me because Jack is very good at only telling you what he thinks you need to know. The other thing that keeps crossing my mind is the night I spent in Jack's bed. I have no memory of it at all and that's *never* happened to me after two glasses of wine. Did Jack lie about how much wine I drank, did he ply me with glass after glass because he knows I'm a pushover after I've drunk alcohol? Jack's a serial shagger and I've always known that but it never bothered me because I'm his friend and I thought that put me out of the loop for his bed-hopping. Did he just fancy sex and I was there so he deliberately got me wasted? I don't know but I need to see if I can find out.

Without actually asking him.

Yet.

I need to find *something* so that I'm sure in my mind that I'm not imagining things or getting it all wrong. I don't know what that *something* is, but I'm hoping that there will be something in his room to give me a clue to what he's been up to.

If he has been up to anything.

I need to ask him how my coat button came to be in a bucket underneath his sink but I know that if I ask him now, he'll just tell me that it must have come off when I visited him weeks ago. He'll lie and be so convincing that I'll end up believing him even though I know I'm right.

I'm sure I'm right.

Almost sure.

He'll remind me how I can't remember things and I'll feel bad for accusing him and I'll doubt myself and end up thinking that it's just something else that I've forgotten. I'm probably wasting my time but I have to try and find something before I ask him.

As soon as he's left the flat for work, I hurry to the window and look down onto the car park below. After several minutes the tall, rangy figure of Jack strides out from the entrance and heads across the car park on his normal route to work. I watch until he's out of sight and then wait ten minutes to be sure that he's not going to come back because he's forgotten something.

I leave the lounge and go out into the hallway and stand outside Jack's bedroom door. My heart is racing and as I put my hand on the door handle, I realise that after I've done this, there is no going back. I'm now about to massively betray my best friend's trust by snooping in his room.

Maybe Olivia wasn't so wrong about me.

I take a deep breath and open the door.

The bed is neatly made and the room is spotless; no clutter or abandoned clothes lying around, no loose change scattered on the chest of drawers, no dirty underpants on the floor. No photographs, no bits and pieces, nothing, the room is as soulless as a hotel room. The only thing that looks slightly out of place in this room is the bed; it's an old-fashioned antique style metal bed frame that doesn't go with the rest of the minimalist room. I wonder if that came from Jack's parents' house, like the pink duvet set.

There aren't many places to search; the wardrobe, the chest of drawers, underneath the bed and the bathroom. I walk into his ensuite and am met with the same pristine neatness as the bedroom. The towels are neatly hanging on the towel rail – folded perfectly and aligned so that the edges are the same level, not bunched up like my own. There is only one bottle of shower gel in the shower and one bottle of shampoo, neatly set side-by-side on the floor. The sliding door on the shower is dry and I think Jack must dry it all after he's used it because he definitely has a shower each morning.

I walk over to the cabinet on the wall over the basin and open it. Two shelves of neatly aligned aftershave, razors and a bottle of men's moisturiser still wrapped in its cellophane stare back at me. I close the doors and look around; there's nowhere else to hide anything so I go back out into the bedroom.

I open the wardrobe doors and instead of the cluttered jumble of my own, hangers are neatly arranged in order; jackets, trousers and shirts. There's a shelf at the top of the wardrobe filled with neatly folded jumpers and sweatshirts and I hold my phone up and take a photograph of them.

I don't know whether Jack will remember where he's put everything but I'm taking no chances. I carefully take sweatshirt and jumper from the shelf and place it carefully on the bed before unfolding them to make sure there's nothing concealed inside. I have no idea what I'm looking for and by the time I've emptied the shelf, I've found nothing. I look at the photograph I've taken and carefully replace everything on the shelf and then look at the chest of drawers.

I pull open the top drawer and carefully feel around the rows of socks that are neatly organised in colours.

Nothing.

I repeat the same procedure with the other two drawers and find nothing except neatly folded underpants and t-shirts. I have a sudden thought that maybe there's something on top of the wardrobe so I stand on the bed so I can get a good look.

Nothing.

I get off the bed and carefully smooth out the duvet and then crouch down on the floor on my hands and knees and look underneath the bed.

Nothing, not even a rogue dust bunny; this man

is seriously clean.

I sit back on my heels and look around the room and face the fact that there is nothing *to* find. What did I expect? What was I actually looking for?

I honestly don't know, just something that would give me some idea of what he's been up to, something that would convince me that I'm not imagining things or going mad.

Or maybe he hasn't been up to anything.

Maybe, Josie, *you've* got it all wrong.

I feel suddenly depressed and dejected; I have blackouts and I don't remember things and that's a fact, can I really be so sure about a stupid button?

No, I can't.

I stand up and look around the room and feel about as bad as I can feel; I'm searching my best friend's room after lying to him that I'm ill. He may be controlling, annoying and moody but what about me, what am I?

I'm a bad person even when I'm sober.

Time to get out of here and hope that Jack never knows what I've done, never knows how little I let myself think of him. I glance around to make sure that nothing is out of place and as I do, I notice a slight imperfection in this immaculate room. One of the cream-coloured finials on each corner of the bed isn't *exactly* straight, it's ever so slightly askew and in this perfect room, it jars.

I walk over to it and study it. It looks as if the finials are separate and screw onto each corner of the bed frame – my bed at Olivia's was similar to this and because the bed was old, the finials were always coming loose if I knocked them when I changed the bed. I take a picture of the bedpost so I can replace it in exactly the same way and then take hold of the finial and gently turn it until it comes free. Once it's free I look at it and wonder what I expected. I return it to the bed end and am about to screw it back on when something catches my eye on the inside of the tubular post. I move closer and turn my phone torch on and point it down the tube and see that there's the end of a piece of string taped to the inside of the post. I put my phone down and poke my index finger underneath the loop of string and gently pull it. I can feel the resistance of something on the end and I keep pulling the string upwards until a tiny bottle emerges from the bedpost.

I hold it carefully in the palm of my hand and scrutinise it. It's half-full of clear liquid and I squint at the tiny writing on the label. As I read the label my hands start to shake and I let go of the bottle and it clangs against the bedstead and for a moment I think it's going to break, but somehow, it doesn't.

I feel bile rise in my throat and I clamp my hand over my mouth and rush into Jack's bathroom. I just get my head over the toilet before I violently vomit every last thing in my stomach into the toilet bowl.

I put my hand up to the handle and pull the

flush and watch as the water swirls around and around until everything is gone. I wipe my hand across my mouth and then rub my eyes as if I can erase what I've just found hidden in Jack's bedroom.

It's so much worse than anything I could possibly have imagined.

Jack, you are not my friend.

CHAPTER TWENTY-TWO

I sit on the bathroom floor and try to calm the thoughts spinning around in my head. I now know that I wasn't drunk the night that I spent in Jack's bed, I was drugged. He must have slipped some of the GHB that I found hidden in his bedpost into my glass of wine and that's why I can't remember a thing about it. The thought of what he did to me makes me dry-heave again. There's nothing left in my stomach to come up and I put my hand over my mouth and breathe in deeply through my nose. As I sit and think about what I've found and what it means, the sensible part of me is aware that I need to get out of here but I can't seem to make myself move.

Eventually, I summon the energy to get up from the floor although my legs are shaking so badly I feel as if I'm going to collapse. I pull some toilet paper from the roll to wipe my mouth and then pull off some more and wipe around the rim of the toilet. I can't leave any sign that I've been in here. I check it's clean and then flush it again.

I go out into the bedroom and across to the bed and pick up the bottle of GHB and carefully lower it back inside the tubular bed post before replacing the finial. Somehow, I have the presence of mind to look at the photograph on my phone to make sure that I replace it slightly askew. I check the room and bed to ensure I've left no evidence that I've been in here and then let myself out of the room and close the door.

Once in my own bedroom I go into the bathroom and brush my teeth vigorously to get rid of the taste of vomit. I turn the shower on and get straight in and have the quickest wash that I've ever had. I'm feeling panicked and try to calm down by reminding myself that I have all day because Jack's at work. I know that I have no need to hurry but I can't seem to quell the feeling of rising panic.

Once I'm dressed, I throw one of my two suitcases onto the bed and open it and begin to fling my clothes inside. All I can take with me is two suitcases because it's all I can handle on my own. I'll leave everything else and come back with my brother Nick to collect it.

Or maybe I won't bother, maybe I'll just leave what's left here because it's mostly crap anyway.

Thoughts of Jack drugging and raping me – and

it was rape, because I wasn't able to give consent – the button, the night of Rafe's wedding and a million other thoughts are tumbling around in my head and I can't make sense of any of it and for now, I don't even try.

All I know is that I have to get out of here and the only place I can go is to my parents.

What am I going to tell them?

I've no idea.

I can't go back to work tomorrow.

I can't *ever* go back to work.

The first suitcase is full and I close the lid and zip it up and drag it off the bed and onto the floor. I throw the other case onto the bed and open it and am chucking the rest of my clothes in when I hear the unmistakable sound of the front door opening. I stop what I'm doing and carefully tiptoe across the room to the bedroom door and stand and listen. I hear the front door close and Jack's footsteps as he walks down the hallway. I look at my watch to see that it's nearly twelve o'clock.

Why the hell is he back? My heart starts to pound and the feeling of panic threatens to overwhelm me and I wonder what I'm going to do.

Logically, there is only one thing to do and that is to front it out. I can't let Jack know what I've found out because I have no idea what he's capable of.

I take several deep breathes and open my bedroom door and step out into the hallway to hear the sound of the tap running and the kettle being filled. I close my bedroom door and stroll into the kitchen and try to behave as if nothing has happened.

'Hi,' I manage to say in an almost normal voice. 'What are you doing home, skiving again?'

Jack turns from the sink and looks at me and smiles.

'Had a dentist appointment,' he says, with a grin. 'Thought I'd come home and see if my flatmate's okay. Got you a Danish from the deli.'

I look at the table and sure enough, there are two paper bags on the table next to two plates.

'Thanks mate,' I say, my voice sounding wobbly. I pull out one of the chairs and sit down because my legs feel as if they're about to give way. 'Not sure if I'm up to eating yet though.'

'Still feeling rough?' he asks, switching the kettle on and then sliding into the chair opposite.

'A bit,' I say.

He takes the pastries out of the bags and puts them onto the plates and pushes one across to me and then takes a huge bite of his own. In four bites he's eaten the whole thing and he picks his empty plate up and takes it over to the dishwasher, opens the door and stacks it inside. I watch him as he makes the coffee and brings it over and places the mugs on the table.

'You should try it,' he says, nodding at the Danish pastry as he takes a slurp of his coffee. 'They're really good.'

'Maybe later,' I say. 'I really don't feel up to it. I

might go back to bed.' I'm desperate to get away from him and back to the safety of my own room. I can hardly bear to be in the same room as him knowing what he's done to me. As soon as he's gone back to work I'm going to finish packing and leave.

'Sure?' he asks.

'Honestly, I couldn't,' I say. 'It was really kind of you but I can't face food at the moment. You have it if you want it.'

Jack takes another slurp of his coffee, puts the mug down and pushes the plate further towards me.

'No, I bought it for you. You eat it.' He stares at me unsmilingly and I force myself to look back at him as if nothing has changed.

'I'm not hungry,' I say.

'Really?' Jack says. 'Because I would have thought after you'd thrown your guts up in my bathroom, you'd be ravenous.'

I stare at him in shock and he smiles a tight-lipped smile.

'How did you know?' I ask, although it doesn't really matter.

'I watched you. There's a camera in my room,' he says. 'But you'll never find it because it's well disguised.'

I gawp at him and try to think of something to say.

'Actually,' he says. 'I have a very good collection of movies, if you get my drift.'

I fight to keep my face impassive. He filmed us. He filmed me.

'You're disgusting,' I say, my voice choking on the words. 'And searching your room was nothing compared to what you did to me.'

'What?' he asks, staring at me in shock. 'I haven't done anything to you, what the fuck are you talking about?'

'You raped me.' I will not cry.

'Josie, how can you say something like that? I've never raped anyone in my life.' The colour has drained from his face and he looks genuinely distraught. For a moment I'm almost fooled by his acting.

'You drugged me, Jack,' I state. 'I didn't have any choice about having sex with you. You know I found the GHB in your bedroom so don't make out you don't know what I'm talking about.'

He shakes his head and drags his hand through his hair.

'No! It wasn't like that, you've got it all wrong. It was a bit of fun. How can you say something like that? You knew exactly what you were doing and you enjoyed every minute of it.'

Does he honestly not believe that he's done anything wrong? Does he think it's acceptable to drug someone and rape them and because they didn't fight back or remember, it's okay? I look at him and feel a millisecond of doubt; *was* I a willing participant and I've just forgotten?

I could watch the video and find out.

The thought pops into my head and I push it firmly away.

'I don't remember,' I state flatly. 'I don't remember anything about that night. I don't remember having sex with you.'

'You don't remember?' he asks, in a gentler tone and I think what a good actor he is.

'You know I don't remember,' I say, fighting back the tears. 'Wasn't that the whole point of drugging me?'

'No,' he says, shaking his head. 'I didn't know that you couldn't remember until you just told me. You seemed so happy the next day that I thought you felt the same way about me that I felt about you. I was so hurt when you sent me that *fuck off* text but I tried not to show it to save our friendship. I thought that you enjoyed the sex but that was all you wanted, that you didn't want a relationship.'

'You slipped it into my drink without me knowing,' I say.

'Josie, it wasn't like that,' Jack says. 'I would *never* do that, you've got it all wrong.'

'Have I?' I demand, my voice dangerously close to breaking.

'Yes, you have. Josie, you *wanted* to take the GHB, it was *your* idea.'

'How can you say that?' I shout. 'Do you really think I'm that stupid? You're such a liar, Jack, why would I want to be drugged so I can't remember anything?'

‘Oh, Josie.’ Jack shakes his head and smiles at me.

‘Don’t *oh Josie* me,’ I shout. ‘You drugged me and then raped me.’

‘NO, I DIDN’T,’ he shouts. ‘We’d had a couple of glasses of wine and I told you that I had some and that I used it now and then, because it’s a bit like ecstasy and gives you a high. You were really interested and said you’d never tried anything like that before. You *wanted* to try it.’

I stare at him in shock.

‘But you’re right,’ he goes on. ‘It’s my fault, I shouldn’t have let you take it, not with your blackout history.’ He rubs his eyes and looks at me with a grim expression. ‘I’m sorry, Josie. I should never have given it to you. It’s all my fault. It’s never affected my memory when I’ve taken it but I should have thought about it, realised how risky it was for you. I’m such a fucking idiot.’

He sounds and looks so convincing.

‘I’m so, so, sorry.’ He leans his elbows on the table and holds his head in his arms. ‘No way would I have given it to you if I’d had any idea what it would do to you.’

‘So why hide the bottle?’ I ask. ‘If it was all so innocent?’

‘Josie, it’s an illegal drug that I bought off the internet. I’m hardly going to keep it on the bathroom shelf, am I?’

I think about what he’s said and everything is whirling around in my head and part of me so wants to believe him because he's my best friend and I don't want to lose him.

'Do you really think I'm capable of rape?' he asks, quietly. 'Do you think so little of me?'

I stare at him but don't answer because truthfully, I don't know. We sit in silence for several minutes.

'So,' he eventually says. 'What were you looking for in my room?'

'I don't know.'

'Come on, you can do better than that. Time to be honest, Josie. Something made you go snooping in my room and I think the least you can do is tell me what it was.'

'Okay,' I say. 'I found a button from my coat underneath the sink and I wanted to know why you had it.'

'A button?' He stares at me and I can see the anger flare in his eyes. 'You searched my room because of a fucking button?'

'I wanted to know why you had it,' I say, sounding ridiculous.

'Why didn't you just ask me?' He stares at me incredulously.

'Okay,' I say. 'I'm asking now.'

He shrugs. 'I have no idea. It must have fallen off your coat when you were here one day, I don't know, it's no big deal, is it?"

'It is a big deal,' I say. 'Because I know that it didn't fall off my coat. I wore that coat the day that I went to Rafe's wedding and it was definitely still attached then. Which means that I must have seen you on that night, the night of Rafe's wedding, and I want to know why you didn't tell me.'

Jack stares at me for a moment and then looks away.

'Tell me,' I demand.

'I can't,' he says, quietly.

'Yes, you can. It's a simple enough question.'

He shakes his head and looks down at his hands.

'Okay,' I near shout at him. 'I think we're done here because you're a liar, Jack. I thought you were my friend but you're just a liar.'

I stand up and Jack looks up at me.

'What are you doing?' he asks.

'Packing my bags,' I say. 'And then I'm going to think long and hard about whether I need to go to the police or not because right now I'm not sure about anything.'

'Don't do that, Josie, please.' He looks at me pleadingly. 'You know I'd never hurt you. I never raped you, you know that.'

'I don't know anything,' I say. 'You can't even answer a simple question about a button, for God's sake.'

'Please, Josie, just let it go.'

'NO!' I turn and head towards my bedroom.

'I was protecting you.' I hear Jack say and I spin around on my heel.

'What?'

'I was protecting you.'

'From WHAT?' I demand.

'From yourself.'

'Explain it to me Jack, or I'm leaving right now.' I walk over to him and glare down at him. 'No more games, no more lies, just fucking tell me.'

'Okay.' He sighs and looks up at me, his eyes searching my face and I suddenly think that maybe I don't want to hear what he's going to say, maybe it's better if he keeps silent.

But it's too late; and a part of me knows what he's going to say before he even utters the words.

'You killed her, Josie,' he says, quietly. 'You killed Evelyn.'

CHAPTER TWENTY-THREE

We stare at each other and my legs start to wobble and Jack jumps up and puts his arms around me and slowly lowers me onto the chair.

'I killed her?'

He nods and I start to cry.

'I don't remember seeing you at all,' I sob, with my head in my hands. 'Tell me what happened.'

Jack sighs and sits back down and then reaches across the table and pulls my hands from my face and takes hold of my hands.

'Okay. I'll tell you. But you have to remember that it wasn't your fault, okay?'

'Okay.'

'You were right, you never came here, I followed you from the church. You didn't even know I was there.'

'What, you followed me? Why were you following me? Why? How did you even know I was going to be at the church? I never told you. I never told anyone.'

'Oh, come on,' Jack says. 'I *knew* you'd be there. It was no secret that Rafe was getting married and I knew you were still obsessed with the prick so I didn't need to be a detective to work it out. I followed you because I wanted to look out for you. I know you, Josie; I *knew* it wouldn't end well and I knew you'd drink, despite having given it up for months. I was trying to protect you.'

'You saw me talking to Evelyn?'

'Yep. It was just rotten luck that you bumped into her. I saw you get thrown out of the church and you were staggering around and the church was only a few streets away from her house so it was just monumentally bad timing. Or maybe you were intending on going to her house, I don't know. I'm surprised you could even manage to walk you were so wasted, let alone find Evelyn's house. Anyway, there she was, walking towards you and you stepped in front of her and stopped her. You were shouting at her and she was laughing at you, said that by Monday you wouldn't have a job anymore and you'd never work again by the time she'd finished with you. She didn't know that I was loitering by the trees, watching. She pushed you away and you went flying onto the ground and she left you there and walked off. She must have thought that was it, but you must have followed her.'

'I did?' My mouth is so dry that I can hardly speak.

'You did, and the silly cow must have let you into the house. Or maybe you pushed your way in, I don't know, I didn't see you go in there.'

'What happened?' I ask, in a whisper.

Jack rubs his hands through his hair, making it stick up in tufts and then he closes his eyes and opens them and takes a shuddering breath.

'I should have been quicker,' he says, with a sigh. 'If I'd got there sooner, I could have stopped you but some old biddy fell over with her shopping right in front of me and I couldn't just walk past her and ignore her because she was about five-hundred-years-old and she was practically begging me to help her up. It never crossed my mind that Evelyn would let you in; I expected to find you wandering the streets in a daze, you were that pissed. I helped the old girl up and made sure she was alright and by the time I got to Evelyn's house, it was too late.'

He looks at me and I see him fighting to control his emotions.

'I couldn't see you anywhere and the front door was slightly ajar and I guessed that you must be in there. As I opened the door to go in, I think a part of me knew what I was going to find before I even got inside because it was so quiet; no shouting, nothing. She was dead, Josie, and there was blood. Fucking hell, so much blood.'

'Dead,' I repeat, and as I say it, a memory of that day stirs, a brief snapshot of a large room with dark furniture and the pervading smell of lavender.

'You'd gone, I searched the house and there was no sign of you but the back door from the kitchen was flung wide open. And your coat was lying on the kitchen floor. I picked it up and brought it home with me and got rid of it because it had a lot of blood on it. The button must have fallen off when I wrapped it up in a bin bag in here. I didn't find the button until the next day so I chucked it in the bucket. I should have thrown it away.'

'Oh God.' I whisper.

He shudders and I feel sick.

'Go on,' I urge. 'Tell me what I did. I need to know.'

'There was this big, metal thing, like a doorstop or something,' he says. 'I don't know exactly what it was because it was covered in blood. You must have hit her with it and she fell. I think her head hit the stone hearth around the log burner as she went down because her head was on the hearth.'

'It was an elephant,' I say, as I suddenly remember. 'An elephant doorstop.' In my mind's eye I see a dark red river of blood spreading rapidly over a rose-coloured patterned carpet and it's as if a jigsaw of that night is slotting into place.

And I know that Jack is telling the truth.

'I'm sorry,' Jack says. 'I didn't want to tell you. I know you didn't mean to do it, you didn't know what you were doing. You were wasted, completely gone. Maybe you just meant to frighten her, maybe it was an accident, I don't know.'

I stare at him and I know that he tried to protect me, that he is, after everything that I've accused him of, a true friend.

'I looked everywhere for you,' Jack says. 'I searched the streets for hours and hours but I couldn't find you and I was so afraid the police would get to you first. Eventually I went back to your flat and waited outside and hoped that you'd eventually find your way back there. And you did.'

'It's okay,' I whisper. 'I'm starting to remember now. I'm sorry you had to do that for me.'

'I've let you down,' he says, squeezing my hands tightly. 'I should have stopped you.'

'Never,' I say, as the tears begin to flow. 'You've never let me down and you've done more than any friend should have to do.'

We sit in silence as I sob, because what else is there to say?

Now I know the truth. I've never allowed myself to remember that night because I couldn't face what I'd done.

I'm a murderer.

* * *

Somehow, I slept.

Jack never went back to work that afternoon, he wouldn't leave me because he was afraid of what I might do. I didn't stop him when he rang Donald and told him that he wouldn't be coming back to work because he'd just had a root canal and it was too painful. I didn't stop him when he curled up next to me on my bed that night and wrapped his arms around me and held me as I sobbed myself to sleep.

We sat in the kitchen for hours, talking about that night, and the more we talked, the more of what happened came back to me. Like most times when I drink, it came back in snapshots; I remember staring at Evelyn's body on the floor and my terror that she was dead. I can see Jack's face as he held me in his arms and tried to calm me down. We were back at Olivia's flat, then, he said, but I honestly had no idea where I was. I don't remember him helping me into bed or clearing up the mess I made when I vomited all over Olivia's kitchen. There is so much that I don't remember and now I've stopped trying to remember, because I want to forget that night and what I've done.

I feel so utterly ashamed that I doubted Jack. He's done more than any friend should ever have to.

Most of the blood from Evelyn was on the floor of her lounge, he said, and he's certain that the fall onto the stone log burner surround was what killed her and not the blow to the back of her head where I must have struck her with the doorstop.

I think he's saying that to make me feel better.

To make me feel less like a murderer.

I thought the police said she'd been bludgeoned to death; doesn't that mean she was hit more than once? I don't know and I'm not going to try and find out because I don't want to know. The parts that I do remember are bad enough. Whenever Evelyn comes to my mind, I push all thoughts of her and that night, firmly away because what is the point of torturing myself with things that I can't change?

Jack said he took my coat and stuffed it into someone else's dustbin a few streets away from the flat. The refuse lorry was on its fortnightly collection a couple of days later and he thought that was the best way to get rid of it. He put it in a bin liner and tied the top up and that was when the button must have come off. Imagine if that had happened in Evelyn's house? It doesn't bear thinking about. He says the coat will be in amongst the thousands of other pieces of rubbish at the municipal tip by now and there is no possibility of it ever being found.

I wish that I'd never found that button.

Because then I wouldn't know what I'd done and I'd be blissfully ignorant.

But I do know, and I have to live with the knowledge that I took another person's life. I would never have done that if I was sober, but the fact that I was drunk doesn't excuse what I did.

When I awoke the next morning, for a moment everything seemed normal, until it all came rushing back and I was desperate to block it all out.

Jack wanted to stay off work with me the next day, too, but I persuaded him to go in because it would look suspicious if we were both absent again. He brought me tea and toast in bed at eight o'clock and sat on the bed and watched while I ate it. He says I have to stop trying to remember that night, because it won't change anything. Evelyn is dead and there's no going back.

Once he'd gone to work, I got out of bed and showered and dressed and tried to behave as if it was a normal day and I hadn't just found out that I'd murdered my boss. I slowly unpacked all of my clothes and put them away and shoved the suitcases back underneath the bed. Every time I started thinking about Evelyn, I pushed the thought away and made a conscious effort not to think about that night. Then I started thinking about Olivia and how she was scared of me and I started to wonder if maybe she wasn't imagining it. Maybe I had been going into her room and I've forgotten that, too.

Maybe I've done other things to her that she was too frightened to tell me about.

This frightened me almost as much as not remembering about Evelyn and I had to not think about that, either, in case I remembered something awful that I'd done to Olivia.

I think I need help.

I said this to Jack and he said I don't need help, I just need not to drink ever again.

Somehow, I got through the day, and Jack

texted me every half-an-hour to check on me. He came home at lunchtime and cooked me a bacon sandwich and acted as if all that we'd talked about on Monday had never happened. If I tried to bring it up, he stopped me and refused to engage. He said it's futile to keep going over and over it, it's done, he said, time to move one.

You make it sound so easy, I said, and he said it is, and I need to stop dwelling on it. You have free will, he said, so use it and never think of it again.

When he went back to work, I cleaned up the kitchen and thought about what he'd said and realised that I have two choices; I can dwell on what I've done and give myself up to the police, or I can pretend it never happened and carry on with my life.

I'm going to carry on with my life.

But that doesn't stop the guilt.

Inside, I'll never forgive myself for what I've done but I can't face a life in prison, I just can't, because I'm weak and I'll break. But that's not the only reason that I'm not giving myself up to the police – I'm not completely selfish.

If I confess, that will implicate Jack and he'll be an accessory to murder.

I can't do that to him, not after what he's done for me, because none of it is his fault, so I *have* to get on with it. Jack says that Evelyn's death is no loss; she has no family to miss her and she was a horrible bitch of a boss, so her death is a blessing in disguise. She may be dead, he says, but at least thirty-eight people have happier lives because she's gone.

So I'm trying to put all thoughts of Evelyn from my mind, and Olivia, too, because I have to start afresh and be a new person. And while Jack was at work, to stop myself from dwelling on it all, I got the vacuum cleaner and dusters out and cleaned the flat until it shone like a new pin. Admittedly, it wasn't even dirty to start with but that wasn't the point, I was keeping busy doing something useful and it felt almost cathartic. I'm going to change my ways and become more like Jack, because there's nothing wrong with being clean and tidy.

By the time Jack came home from work there was a pasta bake cooking in the oven and I'd set the table ready for dinner like a fifties housewife even though, obviously, we're not a couple. The only thing missing was a bottle of wine but I've accepted that I can never touch a drop of alcohol again and actually, that'll be a relief because I'm a different person when I drink and I don't *ever* want to be that person again.

In my head I've apologised to Evelyn and that's all I can do.

I'm going to be a new and better person.

* * *

I went back to work on Thursday; Jack and I agreed that three days would look about right for a flu-type illness. I didn't wear any makeup and my hair was a bit lank where it needed a wash so I looked a bit rough.

Not that anyone was in the slightest bit interested.

It's a fact that most people are so wrapped up in their own lives that they don't have the time or inclination to care about other people's. Even the manager, Donald, barely raised an eyebrow when I gave him my completed absence form. If anyone was off sick when Evelyn ran the department, they'd have to attend a *back to work interview* with her the very minute they arrived back at work. The interview would consist of Evelyn asking endless questions about what illness they'd had, when it started, when it ended and everything in between. Her back to work interviews were the reason why our department had the best attendance record in the whole company. The only person who ever took time off sick in our office was Evelyn. When I went into Donald's office and gave him my completed form, I asked when my *back to work interview* would be and he picked the form up, glanced at it and said the form was good enough and not to worry about an interview.

The *if onlys* started in my mind then; if only I'd had a nice boss and not Evelyn, if only I'd not crashed Rafe's wedding, if only I'd not bought that bottle of vodka.

I allowed myself to think about it for exactly five minutes and then pushed it all away and repeated my new mantra to myself.

No dwelling. Move on.

Jack said he'd caught Darla making a few snide comments about us both being off on Monday but he had a go at her so didn't think she'd gossip about it too badly. That's probably why she was a bit sheepish when she asked me if I was feeling better when I was making a coffee. I don't really care about people gossiping, after what I've discovered about myself and what I'm capable of, everything else seems trivial.

It wasn't until Damien messaged me on Thursday afternoon that I realised I hadn't heard anything from him since Sunday. I hadn't even noticed. The text was brief, asking if I was well and telling me that he was away on business for the next week but would get in touch on his return. Before I found out what I'd done, I'd have been obsessing about Damien and convincing myself that he was giving me the brush off but now, I don't because I have a different perspective on life. It's no big deal, he's away on business and obviously, I won't be able to see him until he gets back. That quite suits me actually, because I need some space to get myself back to normal and practice avoiding thinking about stuff that I can't deal with. I have to be able to do this otherwise the only alternative is to confess everything to the police and go to prison.

I'm starting to wonder if my blackouts when I drink are deliberate; my subconscious telling myself I don't remember so I'm not aware of my terrible behaviour. I don't know if this is even possible but what I do know is that I'm not going to try to remember *anything* anymore, because it won't achieve anything.

I'm going to spend the next week behaving as if everything is normal and if I can do that, eventually it will *become* normal. I'm going to join Jack's gym and get fitter because I need to keep busy, I don't want to sit around and dwell, I have to keep myself occupied. Maybe I'll go out with the crowd from work on Saturday night, because I have to start living otherwise it's all happened for nothing and I might as well just give myself up now.

I'm not even allowing myself to look online at the news to see if there are any updates on Evelyn's murder, because I don't want to think about it. If somehow the police find out it's me, then that's fate and there's nothing I can do about it but as Jack says, it's been seven weeks now and they can't have any evidence otherwise I'd have been arrested.

I have to convince myself that it never happened if I don't want to drive myself insane with guilt.

It never happened, Josie, it never happened.

I just need to keep telling myself that.

CHAPTER TWENTY-FOUR

'What's that you're drinking?' Darla shouts over the pounding beat of the club music.

'Vodka and tonic,' I shout back.

'Ooh, very posh,' Darla shouts, with a laugh. 'I'm sticking to white wine 'cos I'm a lightweight.'

I laugh and when Darla heads to the dance floor, I put my glass on the table amongst the dozens of others on there and follow her. Several of my workmates are already dancing and we join in next to them.

It's not vodka, of course, it's just tonic, but it's easier to pretend that I'm drinking rather than suffer the endless questions about why I'm not. It stops other people constantly trying to persuade me to have a *proper* drink or having them assume that I'm weird for not downing loads of booze. If people are intent on having a skin full, they want you to drink along with them and I can't ever do that again. Not even one glass, because it's a slippery slope.

We wedge ourselves amongst the bodies on the dance floor and I start to move from side to side. I feel self-conscious and awkward without alcohol to give me confidence and I realise how much I've relied on it over the years. I watch as Darla raises her arms in the air and begins to slowly turn around and wiggle. I envy her and feel staid and old-fashioned doing my maiden aunt side-to-side shuffle.

The music track changes and the tempo steps up a notch and the thump of the beat feels as if it's reverberating through the floor and into my feet and through my body. I have to learn to enjoy myself without the prop of alcohol so I close my eyes and imagine that I'm alone and no one else can see me. Gradually the music starts to take over and I begin to dance as if no one is watching me, because with my eyes shut, I can't see *them*. I start to enjoy myself and even though I know there are people all around me, I dance freely and when I eventually open my eyes, no one is watching me because they're all too busy enjoying themselves.

We dance to track after track and I begin to feel a new found confidence.

I don't *need* alcohol anymore.

By the time Darla and I leave the dance floor, we're hot and sweaty and desperate for a drink.

When we reach the bar, Darla surprises me by ordering a coke and feeling that I don't have to lie anymore, I have one too.

'Three wines is my limit,' she says, with a laugh, as we're eventually served our drinks in lukewarm tumblers straight from the glass washer. 'Any more than that and I'm a mess.'

We take our drinks and worm our way through the throng of the club and up the narrow stairs onto the rooftop smoking area so Darla can have a cigarette.

'Too hot in there,' she says, as she lights up.

'Was a bit,' I agree. Although the clouds of cigarette smoke from the group of smokers is hardly refreshing.

'First time you've come out with us lot for ages,' she says, between puffs. 'What made you come?'

'Fancied a change,' I say. 'Got into a bit of a rut and I need to get out and about a bit more and meet new people.'

She nods and I think she's going to ask about Jack, ask if we're an item, but she doesn't. Maybe she's too afraid of him having a go at her again. Jack didn't come tonight because he rarely goes on a work night out and he doesn't want to do anything out of the ordinary. Although he encouraged me to come, said that I needed to start properly living.

'So,' Darla says, flicking her cigarette ash on the floor. 'The police still haven't caught Evelyn's murderer.'

I feel myself flush when she says it and I'm grateful for the dim lighting around the rooftop.

'No,' I agree. 'They haven't. I wonder if they ever will.'

Darla raises an eyebrow at me and blasts away on her cigarette and I will her to hurry up, because it's cold up here on the roof. She takes a last drag and drops the stub on the floor and crushes it with her shoe.

'Who knows,' she says, leaning towards me in her trademark pose for imparting a bit of gossip. 'But I do have some inside info and if I tell you, you've got to promise not to repeat it to anyone.'

I don't want to hear it and I don't want to talk about Evelyn but I can't say no, because how odd would that look?

Very odd.

'I won't say a word,' I promise.

'Well. My cousin's husband is a DCI,' she says, proudly. 'And he's told her some of the things that they don't release to the public. You know, the stuff they keep back so that when all the nutters start ringing up and confessing, they know they're lying and don't have to waste time investigating them.'

She looks at me and I know that I have to encourage her to tell me whatever bit of gossip she has, because this is how Darla works. You have to beg her to tell you, even though she's desperate to blab to the whole world everything that she knows. I suddenly wish that I hadn't come tonight, or at least hadn't ended up sitting with Darla, because now I'm going to have to talk about the very thing that I'm trying to avoid.

She's still looking at me expectantly so I have no choice but to oblige.

'What has he told your cousin?'

'Well,' Darla says, with obvious satisfaction. 'The dog. No one knows about the dog.'

'What dog?'

'Evelyn's dog.' She nods her head and smiles knowingly at the shock on my face. 'Yeah, I know, who knew she had a dog? She kept that quiet, didn't she? Probably didn't want anyone to know that she actually had any feelings for anything. It was a little terrier thing that she used to pay a company to walk for her when she was at work. According to them she absolutely doted on it, treated it like a baby.'

'Really?'

'She did. Spent a fortune on special food for it, it even had a coat for when it was cold. A Barbour.' Darla laughs.

'So where's the dog, now?' I ask, wondering where this is all going.

'Well, that's the thing.' Darla drops her voice an octave. 'Whoever murdered Evelyn, they did the dog, too.'

I stare at her.

'Yeah, horrible, isn't it?'

'You mean..' I start to say.

'Yep.' Darla's voice drops to a whisper and she

looks around to make sure that no one is listening. 'They wrung the poor little bastard's neck.'

* * *

Jack was out when I got home from the club; I was desperate to talk to him about what Darla had told me but I made myself go through the motions of brushing my teeth and getting ready for bed, even though I didn't think there was any possibility that I would sleep. I lay in bed and waited for him to come home, all the while running what Darla had told me through my head. Jack never told me about the dog, and I can see why, because it's just one more horrific thing that I've done without being aware of it.

I don't remember anything about a dog, so I've obviously blocked it from my mind the way I'd blocked everything else. I can't imagine myself strangling a dog, but then I can't imagine myself murdering Evelyn. As I lay in the darkness, I made no attempt to remember because I knew that I wouldn't be able to cope.

I asked myself why killing a dog seemed so much worse than killing Evelyn and I eventually realised why; because from what Jack says, I killed Evelyn in a rage, and maybe it was even accidental, but strangling a dog is cold-blooded and calculated. Was it attacking me? Darla said it was a small terrier so it would hardly have been a threat to me. I don't even have the excuse of it being self-defence.

Somehow, I eventually fell asleep and I don't know what time Jack came back but when I awake on Sunday morning, I can hear him clattering around the kitchen. When I pick my phone up and check the time, I'm shocked to see that it's nearly nine o'clock. For some reason, this makes me feel disgusted with myself, that I can sleep for nearly seven hours when I'm a multiple murderer. A serial killer.

I jump out of bed and go straight into the kitchen in my pyjamas. I need the truth from Jack, every last bit of it, no matter how hard it is to hear and then I have to tell him what I've decided.

'Morning!' Jack smiles at me and opens a cupboard door and gets two mugs out. 'Good night last night?'

I stand in the doorway and don't answer. Jack spoons coffee into the mugs and then turns and looks at me.

'Not a good night, then?'

I shake my head and then immediately start to cry.

'Hey.' Jack comes over and puts his arm around me and holds me tight as I sob into his chest.

'Hey,' he says, loosening his hold and tilting my face upwards. 'A shit night out can't be that bad.'

I stare up at him through my tears.

'You didn't drink, did you Josie?' He asks, concern on his face.

'No.' I shake my head. 'Not a drop.'

'Then what's wrong?'

'Jack, I strangled a dog,' I wail, the words tumbling out in a rush.

'Oh, shit,' he says, pulling me close and holding me tightly.

We stand like this until my sobs eventually turn to hiccups. Jack releases me and pulls out a chair for me to sit on and then sits down opposite me.

'Why didn't you tell me, Jack?'

He shrugs. 'What would have it achieved? It's not like you didn't feel bad enough already. Who told you? Because I've not seen it reported anywhere. I'd assumed they were holding that piece of information back.'

'They were. One of Darla's relatives is in the police and they told her.'

'Big mouth bitch,' Jack says, in disgust. 'She'll open her mouth to the wrong person one day. She couldn't keep a secret if her life depended on it.'

'I definitely did it?' I ask.

Jack nods. 'It was lying next to her, tiny thing, more like a rat than a dog.'

I stare at the floor and imagine putting my hands around its throat and squeezing. There's something wrong with me; Rafe was right, I'm not right in the head.

I need help and I know that I've been fooling myself.

'Jack,' I say, slowly. 'I can't do this, I thought I could, but I can't. I'm going to go to the police and confess.'

'And what will that achieve?' He sighs.

'I can't carry this guilt around. I can't behave as if nothing has happened. I can't live with it.'

'And you think that confessing to the police will make you feel better, that you'll feel less guilty?' he demands. 'You'll feel worse, do you hear me, worse, because you'll be stuck in prison. The minute you've confessed you'll wish that you'd never told them because you won't feel any better. You'll realise that pretending it never happened was far easier than spending the rest of your life behind bars.'

'I'll keep you out of it,' I say, quietly. 'There's no need to involve you, they'll never know you were at Evelyn's.'

'You think I care about *me*?' he shouts. 'This isn't about me, it's about *you*. You're not going to feel instantly better because you confess, you think you will, but you won't.'

'I know I won't, but I can't do it, I can't live a lie. I have to face the consequences and take my punishment. The guilt won't ease because I don't think that will ever go away but at least I can stop lying to everyone else and to myself.'

'This is just a blip, Josie, give it a few days and what Darla told you won't feel so bad. You were fine before she told you and you'll be fine again.'

No.' I shake my head. 'I was fooling myself. Darla telling me about the dog has just bought it to a head. It was never going to work, this pretending that I've done nothing wrong.'

‘Please, Josie,’ Jack says, his voice hoarse. ‘Don’t do this.’

I don’t speak but shake my head. There’s no going back now.

‘You know I love you,’ he says, quietly.

‘I love you, too, Jack.’

‘No, Josie.’ He reaches across the table and cups his hand underneath my chin. ‘I properly love you and not as a mate. I don’t want to lose you.’

‘But I thought, after our night together...’

Jack moves his hand away and laughs softly. ‘I said all that about not wanting a relationship to let you off the hook because you don’t feel the same way. I was saving face.’

‘I’m sorry, Jack.’

‘Don’t be sorry. Just don’t give yourself up, think about it, don’t do anything rash.’

‘I’m not going to change my mind.’ And as I say it, I know that I’m certain that I have to do the right thing and I start to feel a little better, as though a weight is slowly being eased from my shoulders.

‘Okay,’ Jack says. ‘But don’t do it today. Spend one last day with me. We’ll go to the heath, get our walking boots on and blow away the cobwebs. Get a Sunday roast at a pub. Do all of the things that you’re not going to be able to do for a very long time.’ He’s looking at me with a hopeful look in his eyes and I think, why not? One more day isn’t going to make any difference and it’s the least I can do for him after all that he’s done for me. I’ll be saying goodbye to my old life. And to Jack.

'Please?' he says.

'Okay,' I say, 'I'll wait and go to the police tomorrow.'

Jack grins. 'That's my girl. Now go and get dressed and we'll go out for a slap-up breakfast and then walk it off so we've got room for a roast. No soggy toast for us today.'

I stand up and head towards my bedroom to get dressed and then turn back to Jack.

'Jack, I'm not going to change my mind about this. I'm going to the police first thing tomorrow morning.'

'I know,' he says, quietly. 'But just for today, let's pretend it never happened. Have one last day of freedom.'

'Okay.' I turn to leave but Jack's voice stops me.

'Josie?'

'Yes?'

'You won't be on your own, you know, when you go to the police, because I'll come with you.'

I smile and I have to turn away because the tears have started again.

But this time, they're tears of gratitude.

CHAPTER TWENTY-FIVE

I awake to winter sunshine streaming through the curtains and I lie still and try to savour the moment.

This will be the last time that I wake as a free woman for a very long time. I know that once I've taken the step of going to the police station, I'll never be coming back to this flat again and I'll be starting a process that once started, cannot be stopped.

But I haven't changed my mind; I'm going to confess.

Jack and I had a such a great day yesterday, one of the best, and no doubt it was all the sweeter for being my last day of freedom. We put our walking boots and big coats on and walked up into town and had breakfast at Peggy's Café. The breakfast was so huge that I couldn't eat all of mine. Jack finished it off, of course, because he has hollow legs and can eat forever and never put on an ounce.

Stuffed with fried food, we set off towards the heath and proceeded to walk for miles and miles and miles. We didn't once mention Evelyn or going to the police, because yesterday was about spending my last day as a free woman. I was pretending that my life was still normal and I hadn't ruined everything.

Even Jack's confession that he was in love with me didn't make things awkward between us. I think because we both knew that it would be the last day that we'd spend together, we just wanted to make the most of it. I don't know how he can love someone who's committed murder, or stand by me and help me, and I wish that I could repay him in some way, but I can't.

It was already getting dark by the time we left the heath and we walked to an old-fashioned pub called The Cross Keys that I've never been to before, but Jack has, and it was warm and cosy and slightly scruffy. We had to wait for a table because everyone wants to go out for a roast on a Sunday and we hadn't booked, but they fitted us in, eventually, and it was the best roast chicken that I've ever tasted. I realise now how sad it is that I've only fully appreciated the simple things in life, like walking and a good meal, when it's about to be taken away from me.

We walked back from the pub and by the time we got back to the flat, my legs were aching and my feet were sore but I felt happy, in a strange way. I knew that I'd made the right decision and I was beginning to feel at peace with myself.

We settled down in the lounge and Jack insisted on making his *special cocoa*. He said it would help me to get a good night's sleep. I have no idea what was in it but it involved a lot of activity and time in the kitchen and arrived with squirty cream all over the top with a dusting of cocoa powder. We watched trash TV for a couple of hours and then I just couldn't keep my eyes open any longer. All of the walking had properly worn me out. I haven't walked so much in years and obviously, I won't be doing it for a long time and that will be something that I've realised I'm going to miss.

I thanked Jack for a wonderful day and he asked me again, was I sure about going to the police? I told him that I hadn't changed my mind, and I wouldn't go back on what I'd decided and although he looked disappointed, he didn't try to dissuade me again. I tried to make him understand that I felt almost at peace since I'd made my decision and that I knew it was the right thing to do.

He gave me a hug and I went into my bedroom to get ready for bed while he washed up the cocoa mugs – to think that I once found his tidiness annoying, it seems laughable now – and I brushed my teeth and put my pyjamas on and got into bed, fully expecting to lie awake. But I didn't; I fell asleep almost instantly and I slept deeply and soundly, no nasty dreams, in fact no dreams at all, no tossing and turning, until I awoke this morning.

When I woke, I waited for the panic to come rushing in about what's going to happen today, but it didn't. Strangely, I feel calm about what I have to do even though I know that it's not going to be easy. Maybe it's because I've stopped fighting my feelings and stopped pretending and actually made the decision. Jack says that he'll come with me to the police station, but they're hardly going to allow him in to sit in while they interview me, are they? I have to accept that I'm going to be on my own from now on, and I need to get used to it.

I thought about contacting my parents and brother before I give myself up but decided not to. What could I ever say to them that will make any of what's going to happen any easier for them?

Nothing.

There's nothing that can justify what I've done and I don't deserve sympathy and quite honestly, I wouldn't blame them if they disowned me. I haven't been much of a daughter to them, I've barely bothered with them since I left home to go to university. I've treated my visits home as a chore, not a pleasure, as if my parents are a nuisance for expecting the daughter they've lavished love and affection on to visit them now and again.

Too late, I realise what I'm giving up and how different my life could have been if I hadn't been so totally stupid and selfish. I think Rafe was right;

that maybe I'm not right in the head, because normal people don't commit murder, do they?

But none of it matters now because I have to concentrate on today and doing the right thing.

I reach for my phone to see what time it is but it's not on the bedside table. I was so tired last night that I must have left it on the coffee table in the lounge. The battery barely lasts a day so it'll be dead by now and need charging.

But will it? Will I need it, will I even be allowed to have a phone? I don't think I will, because don't people smuggle phones into prison? It'll be one of the many things that I'm going to have to learn to do without. The thought of how different my life will be – can it even be classed as a life? – threatens to overwhelm me and I breathe slowly in and out in an attempt to calm myself. There's absolutely no point in scaring myself with fears of what serving a prison sentence will be like so I have to try and concentrate on the here and now.

I lie still and listen but I can't hear Jack doing his normal clattering around and I wonder if he's still asleep from the exertions of yesterday. I'm guessing that it must be at least eight o'clock because of the way the sunlight is streaming through the curtains. Usually it's still dark when I get up for work at seven.

I wonder what reason Jack will give Donald for not going into work today. Although by tomorrow he'll be able to tell him the truth so I don't suppose anyone will blame Jack for lying about it then. Not that he'll care, Jack has the thickest skin of anyone that I know.

Darla will have a field day with the gossip, it'll keep her going for weeks. Months, even. I wonder what my old workmates will say about me when I'm declared a murderer.

Enough.

It's time I got up.

I throw back the duvet and clamber out of bed. I go straight into the bathroom and turn on the shower and get undressed, trying to put it out of my mind that this is the last time I'll do that here. I get into the shower and vigorously wash myself and try not to think about the horror stories I've heard about prison life. I wash my hair and condition it, too, because who knows when I'll next get a chance.

By the time I've dried my hair the nerves have taken hold. My stomach is churning and I have a metallic taste in my mouth but I tell myself to get a grip, because now is no time to fall apart. I stand in front of the wardrobe and debate what to wear; what is most suitable for confessing to murder? I settle on a pair of black trousers and a long sleeved t-shirt with a cardigan over the top. I take my comfortable black ankle boots out of the wardrobe and put them next to my handbag ready to put on before I leave. Today is going to be a long day and I'll be ending the day in a cell. I wonder if I'll be allowed to have a change of clothes sent in or if I'll be expected to wear the same clothes for several days and then wonder why it should even matter when I'm confessing to murder.

I cross the room and pull the curtains open and take in the view of the streets below for the very last time.

Am I going to mark everything I do for the last time?

Probably.

I plump the pillows and then shake the duvet and lay it neatly on the bed. I don't know what clothes I'll be allowed to take with me to prison, if any, but whatever I can't take, I'll ask Jack to take what's left here to the charity shop.

I walk over to the door and put my hand on the door handle and will my fingers to stop shaking. I can do this. I have to be strong, I don't want to turn into a wreck and drag Jack down, he's done enough for me already.

I take a deep breath and push the handle down but for some reason it's stuck and won't move at all. I attempt to rattle the handle but it remains rigid. I look at it in puzzlement and wonder if, in my state of anxiety, I'm being extremely stupid and attempting to turn it the wrong way. I study the handle and push it downwards, the way I've done every day since I've lived here but it doesn't move; it's definitely stuck. The lock has chosen today, of all days, to break.

'Jack!' I shout through the door. 'The lock's broken on my door. Jack!'

I listen for his footsteps but am met with

silence.

'JACK!' I shout, louder this time, because if he's asleep, I need to wake him. 'Jack!' I bang loudly on the door with my hand, sure that he can't possibly sleep through the noise.

Silence.

There's only one thing for it, I'll have to bang on the wall between our bedrooms to wake him up. I feel bad waking him up when he's obviously tired but there's nothing else I can do. I walk across the bedroom and bang on the dividing wall but all that results is a resounding silence and a sore hand.

I can't understand what's going on and I stand and think; if only I hadn't stupidly left my phone in the lounge, I could ring Jack to wake him up. I'm wondering if I should use a shoe to bang on the door when I see that a sheet of paper has just been pushed underneath the door.

I stare at the sheet of paper and try to make sense of it.

Why would Jack push a sheet of paper underneath the door? I walk across and pick it up and read it.

I'm sorry. I didn't want to have to do this but you leave me no choice. You're locked in. I'll let you out when you come to your senses. You'll thank me later.

I'll see you at lunchtime.

I love you.

Jack.

I drop the paper and rush to the door and bang on it with my fists as hard as I can.

'Jack!' I scream. 'Let me out of here! Let me out! Jack!'

I stand and listen, my breath coming in ragged gasps.

There's no answer.

Only the sound of the front door as it bangs shut.

CHAPTER TWENTY-SIX

I sit on the bed and fume.

How dare he! He's so bloody infuriating and if he thinks a morning locked in my room like a naughty child will make me change my mind, he's very much mistaken.

For the twentieth time since I heard the front door close, I get up from the bed and go to the door and try the handle.

It won't move at all.

I try brute force to see if I can wrench the damn thing off but it doesn't move so much as a millimetre. I go and flop back onto the bed and stare at the door as if somehow, this will change things.

Now when I think back over last night, Jack agreed with me far too easily. I'd forgotten how when he gives advice, he expects it to be taken and doesn't like it if it's not. He thinks he's always right about everything.

But this is different; this is *murder*, not which new mobile phone to buy or which gym to join.

This is something that I have to decide on my own, however well-intentioned Jack's advice might be.

I should have seen this coming and I curse my stupidity for putting myself in this situation. There *must* be some way I can get out of this room.

But how? I can hardly climb out of a window six stories up and the windows don't even open wide enough for me to be able to get through them anyway. They open for only a couple of inches to allow fresh air in and are restricted from opening wider. And let's face it, with my fear of heights, even if they did open wide, there's no way I'd climb out of a window on the second floor never mind the sixth floor.

I pick up the remote control and turn on my TV so I can at least see what the time is.

Eleven-fifteen.

Jack should be home for lunch soon and when he is, I'm giving full vent to my anger. Yes, he's done more than any friend should have to do but he shouldn't have locked me in here. Whether he thinks I'm making a mistake or not, I'm not going to change my mind because it's *my* decision to make, not his.

I flick around the channels and wish the time away. Without my mobile phone I feel lost, and I'm suddenly aware that this is what prison will be like; I won't have any control over my life at all.

I'll be at the mercy of the prison authorities.

Is that why Jack's done this? To give me a taste of what it'll be like?

Maybe it is.

But I'm not going to change my mind. Despite agreeing with what Jack said about confessing not lessening the guilt, I do feel calmer and more at peace with myself. And if locking me in this room was to make me think what prison life will be like then it hasn't worked; it's had the opposite effect because prison is supposed to be a punishment and I deserve to be punished.

I look at the time on the TV and five minutes has passed.

I resume flicking around the channels until I eventually settle on a non-threatening and non-thought provoking cookery programme. I concentrate on it and put all other thoughts out of my mind and forbid myself from looking at the time until the next set of adverts start. I continue in this way until twelve-thirty comes around and then I turn the TV off and sit in silence and wait for the sound of the front door opening.

By quarter-to-two I have to accept that Jack isn't coming home for lunch. Our office lunch break is from twelve-thirty to one-thirty and unless Jack has another fictitious dentist or doctor appointment, he's not coming home.

I pace up and down the room, getting angrier and angrier with each step and then I drag the pillows off the bed and hurl them as hard as I can at the wall. They hit the wall and flop to the floor with a very unsatisfying flump and I totally lose it in my frustration and pick up my boots and hurl them at the door. I feel slightly better when I see that they've left a black mark on the blonde-coloured wood.

I then pick up the pillows and put them back on the bed and put the boots next to my handbag and turn the TV back on.

Two-twenty.

Three hours to go.

* * *

I've had to resort to drinking water from the tap in the bathroom and my stomach is growling with hunger. It's dark outside as I draw the curtains and I wonder where the hell Jack is. It's gone nine o'clock and he's still not back. I'm beginning to worry that he's had an accident because he wouldn't leave me like, without food, locked in my room.

He loves me.

The thought that he's had an accident – been knocked over by a bus or a car and is unconscious – settles itself in my head and refuses to move. If he's in a coma or, God forbid, dead, I could die in this room, the panicked part of me thinks, which could take a very long time because while I have no food, I have water.

I walk over to the door again and pull the handle even though I know it won't move. There are no screws on the plate of the handle, it's made of smooth aluminium and the door hinges are on the outside of the door. The door is solid wood – oak, I think – so there's no way I could cut through it when all I have as a tool is a flimsy pair of nail scissors. I've thought of calling for help from the window but who would hear me up here? We're on the sixth floor and the next door flat is empty and up for sale so even if I make lots of noise, there's no one to hear me.

Calm down, I tell myself, Jack will be back soon, he's just trying to prove a point.

I veer between panic that he's never coming back and has been hit by a bus, and anger that he would do this to me. I continue in this see-saw way for the next two hours before I hear the sound of the front door opening. I leap off the bed and stand by the bedroom door and listen to Jack's footsteps on the laminate floor as he walks slowly down the hallway.

'Jack!' I scream 'Let me out right now.'

He doesn't answer but I hear the sound of him doing something to the door handle and after what seems like forever, the door finally opens.

'Where have you been?' I shriek at him as he comes into view. 'What the fuck are you playing at?'

'Are you hungry?' he asks, calmly, ignoring my question.

'Of course I'm fucking hungry,' I shout. 'I haven't eaten since yesterday.'

'Come and eat then,' he says, turning and walking out of my room towards the kitchen. 'I've got you a takeaway.'

I stomp behind him into the kitchen and see a giant pizza takeaway box sitting in the middle of the table.

'Sit down,' Jack says, taking two plates out of the cupboard.

Hunger gets the better of me and I sit down on the chair, open the box and take out a slice of pizza and ram it into my mouth. One day without food and I'm like a starving animal, what would I be like if I really had to go without?

Jack slides a plate underneath the pizza I'm stuffing into my mouth and sits down in the chair opposite me.

'So,' I demand, between mouthfuls. 'What do you think you're playing at, locking me in my room?'

'I told you in the note, I wanted you to come to your senses and realise that giving yourself up is a stupid idea.'

'You also said you'd be back at lunchtime,' I shout in his face, spitting pieces of cheese at him as I do so. I pick up another slice of pizza and shove it into my mouth and chew angrily on it.

'Yeah, I was, and then I thought that a few hours wouldn't be long enough for you to know what it was like being locked up.' Jack picks up one of the paper napkins that came with the pizza and carefully wipes it over his face to remove the cheese I spat at him. I watch and feel a small measure of satisfaction at my disgusting table manners because I know how pernickety he is.

'And where's my phone? Give me my bloody phone back,' I demand. 'How dare you steal my phone.'

'It's in a safe place.'

'Give it back to me.'

'No.'

I gnaw on the pizza like an animal while I glare at him. Since when did he get to have all of the power?

'I'm still going to the police,' I say, when I start to feel so full that I can't fit any more pizza in.

'Why?' Jack says. 'You think you can cope with being locked up for years when you can't even stand one day of it? You won't have a TV in your cell, you know. Or an ensuite. You'll have to use the toilet in front of someone else.'

Is he right? I really don't know; my knowledge of prison life is only what I've seen on television dramas.

'Being in prison will be different from my so-called best friend locking me in my room like a naughty child,' I say.

'Yeah, it'll be different,' Jack says. 'It'll be a whole lot worse, because you knew I was coming back, you knew it wasn't forever. How do you think it's going to go knowing that you can't leave, that you can't use your mobile phone to ring someone when you fancy it? You can't have a takeaway or a cheese sandwich when you want, you have to eat what *they* give you. You'll be told when to get up and when to go to bed, when to turn your light out. How do you think you'll like that? How are you going to get on sharing a cell? How will you cope with that? Sleeping in the same room as some fucking psycho?'

'I'm going to prison to be punished,' I snap at him. 'It's supposed to be hard, it's not supposed to be a holiday.'

'Well you might want to go to prison, but I don't.' Jack snaps.

'You won't.' I look at him. 'Of course you won't, Jack.'

'I'm implicated,' he says slowly and carefully, as if I have trouble understanding what he's saying. 'I'll definitely go to prison, because I'm a man and they always come down harder on the man. I'll be an accessory to murder and I'll go to prison for a very long time.'

'You're not an accessory and you won't go to prison. I won't tell them you were there because you *weren't*. I'd already left when you got there so I wouldn't even be lying.'

'I picked your coat up,' Jack states.' I *disposed* of it, that makes me an accessory.'

'No, it doesn't,' I shout. 'I'll tell them I chucked it in a random dustbin, they have no possible way of ever finding out that you did it.'

'Forensics,' Jack says, quietly. 'Once you confess, they'll go through all of the evidence from her house, all of the fingerprints, and they'll find mine and that'll be it, I'll be going to prison.'

'My fingerprints will be all over the place and that's okay,' I say. 'But even if they found any of yours, they won't know that they're yours because they haven't got a record of your fingerprints, have they? And they'd have absolutely no reason to ask you for them.'

He shakes his head. 'Once you go to the police, they'll look at everything, they're like a dog with a bone. Who your friends are, where you live, it'll all come out. They'll look at me because you live with me. They'll find *something,* and once they have the tiniest bit of evidence, everything will come out and I'll be going down for years.'

'But they won't, because I'll be admitting I murdered her so why would they keep looking?'

Jack rakes his fingers through his hair and I wish there was some way that I could convince him that he'll be okay.

'No.' He looks up at me and I see despair in his eyes. 'I can't let you do it.'

'Jack...'

'For fuck's sake, Josie, stop being so dim.'

'I'm not! Everything will be fine, just trust me.'

He shakes his head. 'You're just not getting it, are you?'

'What?' I gawp at him.

'*You* didn't kill Evelyn,' Jack says, with a sigh. '*I* did.'

CHAPTER TWENTY-SEVEN

I stare at Jack.

And I laugh.

'I see what you're trying to do. You think that if you say you did it, you'll stop me going to the police?'

'I killed her.'

'You didn't, I did.'

'No. I just made you think you did.'

'What?'

Jack sighs, closes the lid on the pizza box, picks it up and carries it over to the bin, carefully folds the box over on itself and drops it inside the bin and closes the lid.

'I don't understand, Jack.'

'There's nothing to understand.' He returns to his seat and sits down. 'I killed her. She was a bitch and she deserved to die, end of.'

I try to process what he's saying, to make sense of it.

'But I killed her. I remember,' I say. 'The elephant doorstop, the blood everywhere.'

'Fuck's sake, Josie, of course you remember, you were there watching, but I was the one who killed her.'

'No.' I shake my head. 'It doesn't make any sense. Why would you kill her? You're just trying to protect me. I *know* it was me.'

'You didn't do it, I did.'

'No.' I shake my head. 'What reason would you have to kill her?'

'I've told you. She was going to sack you, she said so. She said you'd be lucky to ever work again after she'd finished with you.'

I stare at Jack with my mouth agape and I simply can't take in what he's telling me.

'But why?' I repeat. 'Why? It doesn't make any sense.'

'She wanted to ruin your life. I stopped her because I couldn't let her do that to you.'

I stare at him as what he's saying gradually starts to sink in.

'So why did you say I'd done it?' I ask.

'Because you were suspicious and I had to stop that. You didn't take much persuading either, did you? You really thought you'd killed the old bitch.'

I stand up.

'Where do you think you're going?'

'I don't know, I need to think.' I'm not a

murderer after all. Everything that I'd come to believe about myself is wrong; I'm *not* a murderer. Jack killed her and he made me believe that it was me to save his own neck. If I hadn't said I was going to the police to confess, he'd have let me carry on thinking that I was a capable of murder for the rest of my life.

'What is there to think about? You know the truth now, so you can stop beating yourself up about it. You don't need to go to the police and confess, you're off the hook. You can go back to normal.'

I stare at him and I know that I should be feeling elated; I have my life back. But Jack has just turned my world upside down because he's not the man that I thought he was. He says he did it for me but that doesn't make it okay to kill someone. He says he's my best friend but was prepared to use me to save himself.

'What are you going to do, Jack?' I ask.

'Well, I won't be confessing.' He laughs. 'No way am I going to prison. No, it's not about what I'm going to do, Josie, it's what you're going to do that bothers me.'

'Me?'

'Yeah, you, that's why I let you think it was you. Because I have a horrible feeling that you're going to tell the police what I did because of your weird sense of right and wrong.'

I stare at him.

'Why the dog, though, Jack? Why kill the dog?'

'Really?' He throws his head back and laughs loudly. 'I killed a woman and you're asking why I killed her fucking dog? I killed it because I could, Josie, and because I wanted to. It was trying to bite my ankles so I wrung its scrawny little neck.'

'You lied to me, Jack. You made me think that I'd done it. I could hardly live with myself and you would have let me spend the rest of my life believing I was a murderer.'

'I had no choice, Josie. And anyway, you weren't that cut up about Evelyn, were you? You were more concerned about her shitty little dog than the fact that you thought you'd killed her. And I did say it might have been an accident to make you feel better.'

I think about what he's said and maybe he's right; maybe I did care more about a dog than Evelyn.

'What else did you lie about?' I ask. 'You said that you loved me, was that a lie, too?'

'No.' Jack stands up and takes hold of me by the shoulders. 'Never. I do love you, more than you'll ever know. I did it for you, Josie, I killed her to stop her from ruining your life.' He gazes down at me and he seems so sincere; so *honest.*

'Maybe I didn't want saving.' I stare up at him and he drops his hands from my shoulders and I turn away and walk into the lounge. I feel Jack following behind me and I experience a moment of fear. He's murdered Evelyn; he's a murderer.

But he loves me, he wouldn't hurt me.

I sit down on the sofa, praying that he doesn't sit next to me. I need time and space to think about what I'm going to do and I can't do it with him crowding me.

'You haven't answered my question, Josie.' Jack stands in front of the sofa looking down at me and I look up and try to meet his gaze.

'What question?'

'Are you going to the police?'

'No.' I shake my head. 'Of course I'm not going to the police.'

He sits down on the sofa opposite and studies me.

'How can I believe you?' he asks.

'Because it's the truth,' I say. 'I'm your best friend, I wouldn't lie to you.'

But maybe I am lying, because I don't know what I'm going to do. I don't know if I'm capable of keeping the knowledge of what Jack has done to myself.

'Tell me what happened that night,' I say. 'The truth this time.'

Jack is silent and for a moment I think he hasn't heard me and then he begins to speak.

'I've told you most of it already. I followed you and was watching as you shouted at her and make a complete fucking dick of yourself. She marched off and you staggered after her and followed her to her house, just like I said. The door was ajar, and I followed you in and closed the door behind me. You were in there stumbling around all over the place and that fucking dog was jumping around yapping and Evelyn was laughing and sneering at you. She was telling you that your life at work was finished and if that wasn't bad enough, she had her mobile in her hand to call the police.'

'Oh, God.'

'Yeah, exactly. She was shocked when she saw me come in. I was going to ask her not to call the police and try to reason with her but then I thought, why bother, because it's not like she's going to take any notice. So I picked up the doorstop and walked over and hit her round the head with it before she had a chance to do anything.'

My mouth is dry and I can't speak. Jack looks at me for a moment before continuing.

'I had to hit her a few times before she finally went down. The good thing was, she never had a chance to scream, she just made a grunting noise. Like a pig, which was funny when you think of it, because she was a pig. You stood there watching and I thought you were going to pass out, you were so wasted. And then you pissed yourself in fright because I could smell it. Then that shitty little dog tried to bite my ankle so I picked it up and strangled it. That's when you started screaming.'

I remember screaming and Jack taking me in his arms and me struggling to get away.

'I tried to calm you down and that's when you ran off, you pulled yourself away and left your coat in my arms,' Jacks says. 'I couldn't believe you'd managed to run when you could barely stand up but somehow you did. I spent the rest of the night looking for you and waited at your flat, like I told you.'

'I'm sorry, Jack, that you felt you had to do that for me.'

He shrugs. 'I've told you, I love you.'

'I'm sorry,' I say, again.

'That's why I wanted you to move in here, so I could look after you, stop you chasing that prick, Rafe.'

'I don't need looking after.'

'You do though, because you make bad decision after bad decision. Take Damien, he's another prick but you haven't learnt, have you? You still go after the users, the men who treat you like shit.'

I look up in surprise.

'You know about Damien?'

'Of course, I know,' Jack snorts.

'You saw him dropping me off?'

'What? Yeah I saw. And I'm not a prude, Josie, you know that, but did you have to stay over on the first night? Not very classy, is it? It's no wonder none of them take you seriously. You never learn, do you? Your gushing messages to him were embarrassing, too, less is more, as they say. You should have a bit more dignity.'

'What...'

Jack laughs, bitterly. 'I felt a bit let-down, if I'm honest, because I thought we had something, that night we spent together but then you went and shagged him. I forgive you, though. Because I love you.'

'You read the messages I sent to Damien?' I ask. He must have gone through all of my messages while he's had my phone.

'As you typed them.' He laughs at the look of confusion on my face. 'You know I love you, Josie, but you're a bit thick sometimes. Maybe that's one of the reasons I love you actually, it makes you seem kind of innocent. I cloned your phone and put a tracker on it as well so you couldn't do anything without me knowing about it. I was looking out for you because you can't look after yourself.'

'You cloned my phone?' I gasp.

'Yep. I almost regretted it when I saw your messages to Damien.' He leans across the coffee table and looks at me seriously. 'All joking aside, you hurt me, Josie, you spread your legs for that piece of shit and then came home and lied to me. After all I've done for you.'

'That's why my phone battery died so quickly,' I say, almost to myself. He's been spying on me, he knows every message that I've sent, everywhere that I've been.

He shrugs. 'Yeah, it does do that.'

'How long has this been going on?' I ask.

'A while.' Jack shrugs. 'What does it matter? If I'm honest, you've disappointed me, Josie. I went to a lot of trouble to have you move in here and you could have had the perfect life if you'd just looked at me properly for once, instead of treating me like your big brother. But no, car crash Josie has to go after someone else when she has the perfect man right under her nose. I thought once Rafe dumped you, you'd turn to me and you did, but you still didn't *want* me, did you? Because you were too busy mooning after that prick. I sent those dog shit letters to him to make it look as if you'd done it because I thought it would make you hate him when he blamed you. But it didn't, you were still mad about him and stalking him on Facebook. Pathetic. Maybe I should have treated you like shit and then you'd have liked me a bit more.'

'You sent the letters? Jack, how could you do that?'

He shrugs and laughs and I wonder what else he's done.

'Olivia?' I ask, a sudden thought crossing my mind.

'Oh, you're catching on.' He grins. 'That was just a bit of fun. It didn't take a lot. I took your keys from your bag when we were at work and copied them. I just moved some of her stuff around, stole a few things. It didn't take much to freak her out, to be honest, because she's a neurotic cow.'

'And I suppose you took the bagful of clothes from my wardrobe?' I ask.

'Guilty as charged,' Jack says, holding his hands up. 'Didn't want any evidence left lying around, even if it had been washed.'

I feel as if I'm in some sort of nightmare but I

know that I'm not going to wake up from this one. I need to get away from here, away from Jack.

'So,' Jack says. 'What are you going to do, Josie? Now that you know all of my secrets?'

'Nothing,' I say. 'I'm not going to do anything. I won't tell anyone.'

Jack pulls himself up off the sofa and walks over to the balcony doors and unlocks them. He opens both doors, and the bitter winter air rushes into the room. I shiver, and it's not just from the cold air.

'The thing is, Josie, you're a crap liar and I don't believe you.' He pulls a crumpled cigarette packet out of his pocket and takes out a cigarette and steps out onto the balcony.

'Honestly, Jack,' I say. 'I won't tell a soul.'

He doesn't speak but puts the cigarette in his mouth and after several attempts with the lighter, draws deeply on it and expels a plume of grey smoke into the cold night air.

'Come out here,' Jack says, between puffs. 'It's a beautiful night.'

'It's too cold,' I say. 'Why don't you come back inside and we can talk?'

He doesn't answer but silently smokes his cigarette. I watch him and wonder if I'm quick enough to get to the front door and get it open before he catches me. I sit and watch in an agony of indecision wondering what to do but I dither for too long; he inhales deeply and then flicks the cigarette out into the black night sky where it briefly burns brightly before disappearing.

'Do you love me, Josie?' he asks.

'Of course I do,' I answer. 'You know I do.'

'But not properly, eh? Not like you loved Rafe?'

'You're my best friend,' I say. 'I won't let you down.'

'It's not enough, Josie, it's not enough.' In three strides Jack is in the lounge in front of me and pulling me up from the sofa. He has a tight grip on each arm and he drags me across the room, through the open doors and out onto the balcony.

'Please, Jack,' I whimper. 'You know I hate heights.' I try not to think about how high up we are, how flimsy this balcony feels, how far there is to fall.

'Hey.' He pulls me close to his chest and wraps his arms around me, holding me tightly. 'Don't worry. I love you, Josie, and I'm going to look after you.'

'You are?'

'Yep.' He kisses me on the forehead and puts his mouth close to my ear. 'We'll be happy here together with no one else to distract us, no men circling you like vultures. You can give your job up and stay here. I'll keep you safe. Just you and me, forever.'

'Can we go in now, Jack, please,' I whisper. 'It's cold.'

'Not yet, in a minute. Here, let's get comfortable.' He releases his grip ever so slightly and hitches himself upward and onto the balcony rail. His long legs are stretched forward and his feet barely touch the floor. I try to keep my feet on the ground but he puts his hands around my waist and pulls me upwards and holds me tightly against him. I stare up at the black night sky and then close my eyes tightly, as if somehow, this will help.

'Hey, it's okay,' he whispers. 'There's no need to be afraid, I've got you. Open your eyes. Josie, and look at me.'

I slowly open my eyes and stare up at him. My feet are no longer touching the floor and I can feel the edge of the glass panels of the balcony digging into the top of my feet. I curl my toes upwards and push my feet as far forward as I can underneath the gap that runs between the balcony floor and the glass.

'Josie?' Jack says. 'Will you live with me here forever and forget everything and everyone else?'

'I will,' I say, my voice hoarse. 'We'll stay here together, just you and me.'

Jack sways slightly and the freezing cold wind whips my hair around my head and I feel drops of rain in the air and I think; is this it? Is this how it ends?

'I love you so much, Josie,' Jack whispers. 'And I wish I could believe you, but I don't. I love you but I can't go to prison, I just can't.'

He takes one arm away from my waist and takes hold of my chin before bending his head to kiss me tenderly on the lips.

'I'm so sorry it has to end like this,' he whispers.

He drops his hand from my face and grips the top of one of my arms and I feel his other hand loosen from my waist and takes hold of my other ar. He's gripping the top of each of my arms and I know that he's going to lift me up and throw me over the balcony. I close my eyes tightly and curl my toes underneath the edge of the gap that runs around the balcony but I know it's no use, he's much bigger and stronger than I am. I can feel my feet slipping out from the gap as Jack lifts me and there's nothing that I can do about it.

And then I feel Jack's grip on me loosen and the sudden cold of the concrete floor beneath my feet feels like a miracle. I open my eyes to see Jack swaying as he releases my arms and fumbles to grasp the balcony rail. His eyes are rounded in terror as he attempts to regain his balance and for a split second we hold each other's gaze.

I put my hand out towards him and grab hold of the front of his shirt.

And I push as hard as I can.

CHAPTER TWENTY-EIGHT

I suppose, when you analyse it, I'm no better than Jack.

I lied.

Massively.

I lied to the police, my parents, my work colleagues and every single person who's asked me what happened that night. I justify it by telling myself that Jack died and took his murder secret with him; I didn't sully his name by telling the police the truth about him and what he did to Evelyn.

Accidental death; that was the official verdict on Jack's death, a tragic accident, a moment's inattention, a too casual attitude to the dangers of falling from a balcony. It was in all of the newspapers and even made the nationals so it must have been a slow news day. One low-rent tabloid reported his death with the headline *dying for a smoke*; which was a bit much, if you ask me.

I told the police how Jack always stood on the balcony to smoke, how he had no fear of heights and would often sit on the rail surround as he puffed away. We were chatting, I told them, that night. I was sitting on the sofa about to go to bed and Jack had stepped onto the balcony for his last cigarette of the day. It all happened so quickly, I said, one minute he was there and the next, he was gone. As we were chatting through the doorway, he lost his balance and fell.

And that was it; there was really no more to tell them other than that.

Sometimes I doubt the events of that night and I'm starting to wonder if I imagined pushing him because it seems very unreal to me now. Did I even need to push him, would he have fallen anyway?

I'll never know.

But I do know that it was him or me; if Jack hadn't died that night, I wouldn't be here now.

After he fell, I stood on the balcony in shock and listened to the sickening thud as he hit the ground below.

And then total silence.

I ran back inside the flat and just reached the kitchen sink in time to vomit up every piece of pizza that I'd eaten that night. In my near-hysteria, it crossed my mind that Jack would have been very pleased about that, being such a neat-freak.

I waited, and expected, police sirens and

ambulances but of course there was none of that because it was dark and past midnight, and no one, except me, saw Jack fall. Things would have been much different had it happened in the daytime and possibly, someone would have seen us on the balcony and there could have been witnesses.

But, luckily for me, there was no one to question my story.

Before I could call the police I had to find my phone, which was easy as it turned out, because it was in Jack's coat pocket. I was a mess on that phone call, barely coherent, gabbling that there'd been an accident and somehow managing to give them the address of the flat. They came very quickly and an ambulance arrived with them. Obviously, the ambulance wasn't needed but I suppose that's procedure, just in case Jack was still alive. By the time they all arrived I was downstairs in the car park kneeling on the floor next to Jack, who was most definitely dead, and I was hysterical. They dragged me away from his body and the paramedic gave me some pills to calm me down. I don't know what it was he gave me, but it calmed me and I felt as if I was watching another person answer the policeman's questions although, obviously, there wasn't much to say. The police insisted that I needed someone to stay with me that night so I lied and told them that I'd rung my brother and he was on his way. They accepted my lie easily, because it was one less problem for them to deal with.

Even now I try very hard not to think about how Jack looked that day and what the brutality of a fall from six storeys high does to a body. I prefer to remember him as he was when he was alive. Before he turned on me, of course.

And most of the time, I succeed.

When the guilt surfaces, just as it did when I thought that I'd killed Evelyn, I remind myself that if Jack had had his way, I would have been the one lying broken and twisted in that car park, and not him.

It was self-defence and realistically, I don't think I could have saved him because he was so much bigger than me and if I'd tried, I'd probably have gone over the balcony with him.

That's what I keep telling myself and most of the time, I believe it.

One thing that I learned from Jack is that I have to move on; if I obsess over this then I might as well confess to the police right now and tell them everything. I don't know it they could call what I did murder, but I have no intention of finding out. It seems so strange that I was so certain that I was going to confess to Evelyn's murder. Now I'm not so sure, when it came to it, whether I would have actually gone through with it.

I'll never know now, what I would have done.

I feel sad that Jack is dead but he *was* going to kill me, so there is that. And even though he said he loved me, it wasn't proper love because he wanted to control me and tell me what to do. He was also happy to let me think that I'd murdered Evelyn and would have let me carry on thinking that if I hadn't been so insistent on going to the police. I also think that the things that he told me he'd done were just the tip of the iceberg. Since he's died, I've discovered other things about Jack that don't add up and even now I think there are many secrets that he took to the grave. I've even begun to wonder if Evelyn was his first victim or if there had been others before because he didn't seem at all bothered about killing her or her dog.

The police wanted to see his mobile phone that night, because they wanted to check to see what he was Googling just before he died so that they could definitely rule out suicide. I told them that I didn't know where it was and they said not to worry but they would come back for it the next day.

Of course I knew where it was but I had things I needed to do before they took it. Luckily, I knew Jack's code for his phone so I could open it. I found videos on his phone and I made myself watch the one of the night we spent together and it was sickening. I was practically unconscious and even though it was technically rape, I felt ashamed and dirty and that, somehow, it was my own fault.

There were other videos, too, some the same as the one of me, and others where the girls were actively participating and he hadn't drugged them. Or maybe he had, but with something different.

I deleted every one of them.

I could have left them on the phone as evidence

and told the police the truth but really, what was there to be gained? Months and possibly years of giving statements, going to court and endless newspaper stories about it – I just couldn't face it. I don't want to spend the rest of my life being seen as a victim of the notorious Jack Davies. And how many police and jurors would have to watch the video of Jack raping me? Far too many. No, it was unthinkable and by deleting those videos, I not only saved myself from that horror but all those other girls, too.

So, in Jack's own words, *it's done, end of*.

I deleted the tracker from my phone and his phone, too, and that was a shock, he'd been tracking me for *months*. Another thing that I found out was that Jack doesn't own a car and never has done – in fact, he doesn't even have a driving license. I've come to the conclusion that he stole that car simply to help me move my stuff into his place and to impress me in some way. I think that's why he was gone for so long once he'd dropped me off at the flat; he was parking that car somewhere far away so that it couldn't be traced to him.

I'm going to have to move out of the flat because I can't afford the rent on my own and it's not as if I want to stay here, anyway, after what's happened. The landlord was quite nice about it when he was informed of Jack's death, he let me stay an extra few weeks while I found somewhere else to live. He didn't even ask for any rent, and I didn't offer any, so that was a bonus. Luckily, one of Darla's many relatives has a spare room that she wants to rent out so I'm moving in this weekend. Darla's going to help me move my stuff in her car, which is really kind of her, and despite her being a gossip, we've become quite friendly these last few weeks. I suppose she's what you'd call a proper friend now, and as long as I don't tell her anything that I don't want the whole world to know, we'll get along fine.

It's amazing how people rally round and want to help when you've experienced the traumatic loss of a friend and I've found it a comfort going to work, rather than a chore. Donald, the manager, might be a dry old stick but he had the foresight to move the office desks around while I was on compassionate leave so that I'm not sitting opposite Jack's empty desk. My desk is next to Darla's now. He also gave everyone the whole day off to attend Jack's funeral. Everyone went, including Gareth Heath, the Marketing Director and a couple of HR flunkeys and of course, Donald.

Not everyone went to the wake at a local hotel though, about half the office disappeared as soon as the service was over and I know a few of them were making an early start at the *Dog and Gun* because the funeral was on a Friday. I made a point of speaking to Jacks's parents and telling them what a great guy he was, but truthfully, they didn't seem particularly interested and I think they were waiting for a suitable amount of time to pass so that they could leave the wake and go home. They were quite old, and well, cold, I suppose, and I remembered then that I'd rarely heard Jack speak about them, and that he hardly ever visited them. So that was it, the funeral was over and in just a few weeks, Jack is hardly mentioned by anyone at work and I know that in few months it'll be as if he'd never been there.

Damien contacted me when he heard about Jack and we met up for a drink. It *was* my suggestion that we met up, I'm not going to lie about that because if nothing else, I have to be honest with myself. I knew that Damien couldn't really refuse to meet me, what with me being a grieving friend and maybe that was a bit naughty of me but I was desperate to see him. And when I turned up at his place a couple of days later and surprised him, although he didn't seem that thrilled at first, I didn't have to exactly force myself on him, if you know what I mean.

Damien has told me that he doesn't want another relationship just yet, because he's still getting over his jealous ex and her controlling ways. He says he wants to be honest with me and that he just wants a bit of fun with no strings attached and no commitment.

Friends with benefits.

I didn't tell him that I don't *do* friends with benefits, because sometimes, things are better left unsaid.

He says that he's not sure he ever wants to commit again, and isn't sure if he's even *capable* of committing to anyone ever again. I can't deny that

I was disappointed when he said it but I tried to hide my disappointment because I didn't want him thinking that I wanted a proper relationship.

Even though I do.

The thing is, I've realised that for me, Damien is the man that I've been looking for all of my life. I know now that what I had with Rafe was *nothing* compared to what Damien and I have. I tried to rush things with Rafe when I should have taken it more slowly. If I hadn't been in such a hurry things wouldn't have turned out the way they did. Sometimes, with men, you have to give them time to be able to cope with their feelings, almost tell them how they feel. I know that Damien and I are absolutely perfect for each other and I can see our future mapped out so clearly. It's just a matter of time before he realises what we have together, so I'm going to be patient and this time, I'm not going to mess it up.

Damien is definitely the *one*.

He just doesn't know it yet.

THE END

Made in the USA
Las Vegas, NV
31 July 2022

52502385R00157